MARIONETTE

MARIONETTE

Margaret James

ST. MARTIN'S PRESS
NEW YORK

Library of Congress Cataloging in Publication Data

James, Margaret.
  Marionette.

  I. Title.
PZ4.B4734Mar 1980   [PR6052.E533]   823'.9'14   79-8445
ISBN 0-312-51524-3

Acknowledgments

My grateful thanks to the authors of the following books, both informative and fascinating, which made it possible for me to write this novel:

The Bankside Book of Puppets H.W. Whanslaw; *Puppets into Actors* Olive Blackham; *Everybody's Marionette Book* H.W. Whanslaw; *London Labour and the London Poor* Henry Mayhew; *Handbook of English Costume in the 19C.* C. Willett Cunnington & Phillis Cunnington; *The Victorian Home* Jenni Calder; *Life Below Stairs* Frank E. Huggett; *Victoriana* James Laver; *Not In Front of the Servants* Frank Dawes. My thanks also to Mr K. Barnard, of the famous family of puppet masters, who furnished me with useful information.   P.B.

MARIONETTE

Prologue

Dora Jones took a last look round her bedroom. Ten o'clock on a cold October night, with nothing in the tiny grate to off-set the chill.

It was almost time to pay a final visit to her mistress, making sure there was no more that she needed before Dora had to tackle the pile of mending which awaited her. The ladies of the house might be able to relax at that hour; mere companions had to work on and earn their keep.

Slowly, Dora pulled her shawl tighter about her, one hand tucking a strand of hair into place as she made her survey. It wasn't bad. In fact, it was really quite good, considering that this was an age when even the most prosperous and charitably-minded of employers were wont to allot to their staff, dark and dirty attics in which to lay their heads.

It was true that the curtains were patched, but their faded rose pattern was still cheerful, and there was even a thin carpet underfoot. She had been given the privilege of a painted wardrobe, long since discarded by the family, in which she put her black serge every night. She only had one other gown; a deep red velveteen which had seen many years of service, but it was nice not to have to hang it behind the door. The wardrobe gave her a certain status. She glanced at the bed, the coverlet a patchwork miracle made by her grandmother which she took everywhere she went; the brass rail and knobs which she had polished until they looked like gold.

No, it wasn't the room which was troubling her, nor was it the lack of warmth. It was something about the house itself;

something odd, which she had sensed as soon as she had entered it some three months before, and which even now she could not explain.

She had told herself many times that she was foolish and ungrateful. She had been lucky to get a position with M. and Mme. Boussard, even if her bedridden mistress was rather peculiar. Their residence in the leafy suburb of Balham was comfortable and well furnished. There was an ample staff for what had to be done; the food was plentiful. Her employers hadn't even commented on the fact that she limped, and was not as nimble on her feet as she should have been.

But it hadn't made any difference. Gradually the feeling of dread had grown deeper, until now Dora was almost afraid to go down the back stairs, or walk along the corridors. There were numerous gasoliers, but they weren't always alight, and she could never be quite sure whether or not it was just imagination which made her think she saw doors ahead of her closing gently, although there had been no sign of anyone in the passages a second before.

She pulled herself together with an effort. She was being ridiculous, and Mme. Boussard would be scathing if she were kept waiting any longer. There was nothing wrong with the house. It was simply that she, Dora, had not settled in. Not important enough to be given the special treatment accorded to a highly-skilled lady's maid, despite the fact that Dora called herself nurse-companion, nor yet lowly enough to be admitted into the warm camaraderie of the rest of the staff, she was on her own. Neither fish, flesh, nor good red herring, but she'd get used to it, and perhaps before long madame would allow her to carry out real nursing duties, instead of insisting that these intimate functions be done by the housekeeper who had been with her for years.

Her hip was paining her more than usual. She'd been up and down stairs countless times that day, and the damp weather didn't help, but she'd learnt to live with pain.

She picked up her candle, worried because it was down to its last spluttering inch. It would just get her to the first floor, if she hurried. She opened the door and then stopped dead.

"Yes? What is it?"

The shape in the doorway had no lamp or candle. It was as if it had come up the attic stairs like a cat which could see in the dark. Dora backed away, her mouth shrivelling to dust as she repeated the question through parched lips.

"What is it? What do you want?"

She knew the light was being taken from her shaking hand and doused, the blackness closing about her, thick and tangible like a blanket. Then she heard a sigh as the door swung to, blowing shut in the draught.

She couldn't stir, and even the faintest scream was beyond her. She felt as if she were turning to stone, locked away from the rest of the world with something which didn't move or speak.

As her heart began to pump with a violence which threatened to choke her, cold and unexpectedly strong fingers reached out and fastened themselves firmly about her wrist.

One

On the 30th January, 1874, Regina arrived at No: 7, Chantry Close, Balham. The journey from her hotel near Piccadilly had been slow, for the roads were covered with treacherous ice, powdered with snow which had been falling for the last two hours.

The coachman was swearing to himself as the horse's hooves slipped, but Regina didn't mind. The wool jacket was thick and expensive, the furs cosseted her. Even her finger-tips were protected, tucked snugly into a sable muff.

There were a lot of things to see: a milk cart, brightly painted and shining with gleaming brasswork; a stout muffin man with a tray covered in green baize balanced on his head, shouting enthusiastically of his wares; a brief glimpse of an apothecary's shop, with its highly coloured bottles of blue, yellow and red; a sweetshop, fleeting by, windows crammed with enticing trays of hard-bake, candied almonds, and sugar plums. There were errand boys whistling and sliding as they went on their way; stout matrons holding on to their bonnets, with wicker baskets on their arms; a few men in dark frock coats and top hats, trying to look dignified despite their red noses and watering eyes.

There was even a tired looking woman selling lavender, her ageing face reflecting her despair. Who would come out of their houses on a day like this to buy the fading bunches tied up with twine?

Regina, aged twenty-one, almost stopped the coach. She felt so sorry for the woman; guilty, when confronted by such poverty and misery. Then common sense prevailed. She was late already, and besides, the driver wouldn't thank her for delaying him further in this appalling weather.

She sat back against the worn leather seat, a small fashionable hat tilted over hair so fair that it looked almost silver. It made her blue eyes seem brighter than stars, complementing the porcelain skin which had a faint blush along the cheekbones. One of her beaux had promised to write a poem to the beauty of her lips; another, not to be outdone, had sworn to pen an ode to the perfection of her nose. Regina had laughed at the pair of them, and the verses had never been written.

When the door of No: 7 opened, Regina nodded to the tall girl with untidy brown hair pushed up into her cap. She had a surprisingly good figure under her black dress and starched apron, and her hands looked well scrubbed.

"I'm Regina Curtis, and I've come to see my aunt and uncle, M. and Mme. Boussard. They aren't expecting me, but I hope that that will not matter."

Effie McGee, the parlourmaid, stepped back at once, recognising quality when she saw it and moved by the caller's smile which seemed to embrace her with its warmth.

"Of course, Miss." Effie ducked politely. "This way, if you please. I'll tell master you're 'ere."

Regina was shewn into the sitting-room, where a fire was piled high in the wrought-iron grate. She moved towards it, drawing off long suede gloves as she looked round with approval. Although Mme. Boussard was bedridden, and thus could not enjoy her feminine sanctuary, it had been furnished just as if she would be appearing at any moment to bid her guest sit down and take tea with her.

There was a gay, sprigged paper on the wall; a Wilton carpet of soft blues and pinks; alcoves by the fire which had been shelved to accommodate porcelain and silver ornaments; a few good water-colours in narrow gilt frames depicting the English countryside.

The furniture was dainty too: brocaded sofa and chairs, with a table or two of pâpier-maché, and a few stools covered with Berlin work.

It was several minutes later that Regina's brows met in a slight frown as an unaccountable shiver went through her. It wasn't that she was cold; the flames were high, roasting her cheeks as well as the hand stretched out to the blaze. It was as if there was a presence in the room, watching her, waiting for her to move.

She shrugged the ludicrous notion away. It was because it was so quiet, of course. The house was on the edge of the suburb, and Chantry Close itself comprised only seven houses, each well separated from its fellows by large gardens and tall trees.

She had no time to dwell further on the curious feeling, for the door was opening to admit a man of some fifty years, slightly bent, with greyish hair worn rather long. His beard and moustache were neatly trimmed, his skin lined and dry, giving him a frail look as if he had been ill.

"Uncle Louis?"

Regina rose at once, tentative, and not certain of her welcome.

"My dear!"

Louis Boussard crossed the room and took her hands in his, kissing her on both cheeks. It felt as if a butterfly had caressed her, so light was the touch, and then Louis was settling her back in her chair, his obvious delight dispelling her fears.

"Regina, what a wonderful surprise! We had no idea that you were in England."

She still looked guilty, her explanation a trifle hurried.

"No, it was very remiss of me not to let you know; do forgive me. To tell you the truth, my visit to England was a sudden decision. I've only been here for two days, but I felt I had to come and see you and Aunt Marionette as soon as I could. I should have written to you, of course."

Louis brushed aside her contrition and pulled the bell-cord.

"Nonsense, what does it matter? You're here, and that is what counts." He eyed her with approval. "And to think that this is the first time we have ever seen Yvette's daughter, and such an enchanting one too."

Regina blushed.

"I know, I should have come before, but when my mother and father died ..."

"Of course, of course." He leaned forward, patting her hand. "There is no need to explain. After all, we haven't been to France for years, so why should you come to England?"

"How is Aunt Marionette?"

M. Boussard's pleasure faded as he shook his head.

"She doesn't improve, I fear. I expect you know what happened. You have been told of the accident?"

"Yes." She was as sober as he, watching the pain in him. "A coach overturned I believe."

"Yes. Marionette and her father, Jules Marigny, were on their way to London, where he was to give one of his puppet shows." He glanced up. "You'll also be aware, I'm sure, that Jules was one of the greatest puppet masters of our time."

"Yes, indeed."

"Well, as you say, the coach overturned. Jules was killed instantly, and Marionette badly injured. That was twenty years ago; she has never walked since."

"There is no hope?"

"None. She will be like that for the rest of her life. Oh good, here is Effie." He blinked a trace of moisture from his eyes as he turned to the maid. "Effie, some tea please, and tell Mrs Pritchard that Miss Curtis has arrived." He looked back at Regina anxiously. "You'll stay, of course? Just for a few days at least. Oh please do say yes; it would give us such joy."

"I don't want to inconvenience you. I could easily go back to town."

"We won't hear of it. Effie, tell Mrs Preece to get a room ready. Off you go."

They talked for a while. There seemed to be an instant rapport between them as Louis asked eager questions about Paris, and told Regina something of his own household.

"Marcelle is Marionette's cousin." He was a trifle wry. "You won't have met her, naturally, but doubtless your parents told you about her. She made a bad marriage, so the family thought. She has lived here now for seven years with her husband, Denys Pritchard, and their two children, Victor and Jeanne. Poor little Jeanne."

Regina gave him an enquiring look, and he sighed.

"Jeanne is dumb. She was very ill when she was thirteen; some kind of fever. She's sixteen now, and she hasn't spoken a word for three years. Sometimes she makes noises as if she's trying to tell us things, but it's no good. She can't talk."

"How awful!"

"Yes, it is." Louis hurried on, as if he didn't want to dwell on the girl's misfortune. "We've another guest at the moment too, a Herr Von Heltz. He's come to collect material for a book on old buildings. You'll see him later." He got up as the door opened. "Marcelle, come and meet Regina. She's Yvette's daughter, you know, and isn't it nice to have her with us?"

But if Louis Boussard was glad to see her, Regina was sure from the very first moment that Marcelle Pritchard was not. She was a well-built woman, with red hair frizzed into a bold fringe low on her brow, favouring hard bright colours for her gown which did nothing to enhance her own rather high complexion. As she walked, she jangled with a miscellany of necklaces and bangles, her fingers toying with a string of jet beads as she took a seat opposite Regina and considered her with set lips.

The shock of finding the girl there was two-fold. First, she had always hoped that Yvette's daughter would never come to England. Jules Marigny's fortune had been left equally between his two daughters, but when Yvette Curtis died, her share reverted to Marionette. Since it was likely that Louis would die at roughly the same time as Marionette, if not before, Marcelle had great hopes that she and her son would inherit a goodly portion of the wealth. Now, with Yvette's daughter here, Marionette might well change her Will, feeling that her dead sister's child was entitled to her mother's legacy.

Secondly, Marcelle, now nearing middle-age, was affronted by the beauty of the newcomer. It was like a blow in the face, and her small mouth grew more petulant still as she said acidly:

"Well, so you've come at last. How long will you be here?"

Regina sensed the hostility, waiting until Effie had put the tray down in front of Marcelle and left the room before she answered.

"Not long. Uncle Louis has asked me to stay for a day or two.

Then I shall go back to London for a while before I go home."

"What made you come?"

"Marcelle!" Louis was unhappy, giving Regina a quick, reassuring glance. "Why shouldn't she come? She's part of our family."

"A fact that she has remembered somewhat belatedly." Mrs Pritchard ignored Louis's distress as she handed him his cup. "Marionette has been lying up there for years, yet no one has troubled themselves to come from France to see her before."

"Well, I'm here now." Regina refused to be ruffled as she sipped her tea. It wasn't difficult to read Marcelle's resentment, but she wouldn't · be at Chantry Close long enough for the woman to become a problem. "May I see Aunt Marionette after tea?"

"Of course."

Clearly, Louis was glad to get the conversation out of Mrs Pritchard's hands, and when the tray had been removed, and Marcelle had taken herself off, cheeks redder than ever, he said comfortingly:

"Don't mind her. She's not a happy woman."

Regina was considering whether it would be wise to enquire why that was, when she became aware that Louis was trying to say something else, which was obviously difficult for him to put into words.

"What is it, uncle?" she asked gently. "Is anything wrong?"

He looked up, studying her face for a long while before he replied.

"I ought to tell you. I don't want to, but it wouldn't be fair for you not to know."

"Know what?"

"It's not easy to explain."

"I'm a good listener."

"I'm sure you are, child, but it's still hard." He took a deep breath, bracing himself against the inevitable. "You see, there are whispers. Rumours, if you like."

"Rumours?" Regina was startled. "What kind of rumours?"

Boussard was more disturbed than ever, rubbing his hands

together as if he were trying to cleanse them of something.

"About Marionette. People say she is strange. It's nonsense, of course, but some think she has unnatural powers."

It was a jolt, and Regina could feel the colour draining from her face. Now, in spite of the fire, her hands were chilled.

"Unnatural powers? I don't understand."

"No, of course not, how could you?" He bit his lip. "It's all so silly, but they think she can do things which other people cannot do."

"Lying in bed?"

"Quite. I told you it was ridiculous, but that's what they say. I wouldn't have mentioned it, but if you stay here, even for a short time, you're bound to hear the gossip. Better to be forewarned."

"Yes, of course."

As Louis rose stiffly from his chair, Regina stood up too, still at a loss. She was not entirely sure what Louis meant, but it had been enough to make the unease she had felt some hours before creep back into her bones. Unnatural powers? A bedridden woman?

When they reached the hall, a man was coming down the last few stairs. He was tall, spare and neat in a dark coat, with a slit of a mouth, hollowed cheeks and black, wavy hair. He nodded distantly, and Louis said meekly:

"This is Dr Morse, Marionette's physician. Dr Morse, my niece, Miss Curtis."

Vernon Morse's slate coloured eyes considered Regina for a brief second, then he inclined his head once more, wholly disinterested.

"Uncle Louis tells me there is no hope that my aunt will ever walk again," said Regina after a long pause. She thought the doctor morose to the point of rudeness, and was determined to make him speak. "Is that really so? Can nothing be done?"

"Nothing." Morse's voice was like a rasp as he took his cape and walking-stick from Effie. "She's had the best treatment available. No use. She won't walk again."

"He doesn't mean to be impolite." Louis always seemed to be apologising. "It's just his manner."·

He waited until Effie had made her way through the green baize door leading to the kitchen below, and then looked back at Regina.

"Well, shall we go and see your aunt? Dont' be alarmed, for I'm sure she will be as happy to see you as I am. I'm certain that she would never do anything to hurt you."

Regina followed Louis Boussard with increasing trepidation. His reference to rumours had not been encouraging. The half-hearted assurance that Marionette would do her niece no harm was even more perturbing.

Daylight was fading, but no one had thought to turn on the gasoliers in the hall. Looking downwards, Regina could have sworn that she caught a glimpse of a small object moving about. A cat? No, it wasn't a cat. Cats weren't coloured like that.

She concentrated on the thick Turkey carpet, putting the nonsense out of her mind. Best quality, with the walls covered in heavy flocked paper of deep crimson. On the landing, which ran the width of the house, there was a series of mahogany doors, all firmly shut against intruding eyes, tables outside each one, ready for the maids to rest the morning tea-trays on them.

It was obvious that a great deal of money had been spent on No: 7, but beneath its rich façade there was an element hard to pin down. Regina shook herself again, scolding herself for her fancies. It was because it was so silent; that must be it. After the noise of central London, it was deathly quiet, only Louis's laboured breathing breaking the stillness.

But what about normal household noises which one might expect? The place was not empty; there were others about. Why couldn't she hear them?

She had no more time to worry about that then, for Louis was throwing open a door, and a second later Regina was in Marionette's room.

She paused for a fraction of time, the knot in her stomach tightening a further degree. Whatever the weird atmosphere was, it was stronger here, despite the luxury of velvet drapes, old rosewood furniture, and a profusion of silver and crystal ornaments on the dressing-table.

It took every bit of Regina's self-possession to cross the room, stopping a foot or two from the bed as she stared down at its occupant.

Marionette Boussard sat bolt upright, propped against half a dozen pillows edged with lace. Her face was colourless, dark hair pulled tightly up into a flat bun on the top of her head. Her eyes were black and unwinking, and from the left lid an ugly scar ran down the cheek, pulling up the corner of the mouth in what appeared to be a permanent grin.

Regina forced herself to remain calm, obeying the wave of Mme. Boussard's hand, moving forward again reluctantly.

Marionette looked her over for another whole minute before she spoke.

"Mm, so you're Yvette's girl, are you? Not like her, nor your father, that Englishman, come to think of it."

"No, I know."

Regina felt gauche, not knowing what to say, but Marionette did not appear to notice. She nodded in the direction of the woman by the window, plump and solid in black bombazine and white apron, a bunch of keys dangling from her leather belt.

"This is Loveday Preece, my housekeeper; she looks after me."

Mrs Preece curtsied, her clumsily formed features immobile.

"Pleased to meet you, Miss. Now, if you'll excuse me, it's time I got madame's tea."

Marionette gave a short laugh as the door closed behind Loveday.

"Ugly as sin," she said briefly and without charity, "but she serves me well. Come a bit closer; let me look at you properly."

Regina hesitated, wondering whether she should proffer a kiss. She half-bent, when the woman in the bed said harshly:

"Don't touch me! Don't ever touch me. If you do, you'll never be the same again."

Regina stiffened, giving Louis a nervous glance. He was staring down at the carpet, uncomfortable and ill-at-ease. She could feel her own tension mounting as she said finally:

"I'm ... I'm sorry. I didn't mean to ..."

"It's all right." The mumbled words were brushed aside. "Just remember what I say."

"Yes, I will."

Regina made a furtive backward move, trying to avoid the unwavering stare. No wonder people whispered about Marionette Boussard. There was something very unusual about her.

"It's snowing again," said Louis, as if he were impelled to make some comment to ease the situation. "See it's quite heavy now."

Regina glanced at the window. Louis was right. The delicate flakes were like a blinding cloud beyond the Nottingham lace screen, yet it wasn't the snow which made a fresh quiver run through her, but the sight of a large black crow perched on the sill. If she hadn't been so close to the window, she wouldn't have seen it in the half-light, preening its feathers, unconcerned by the cold. She had no idea why the sight of it produced the *frisson*. It was only a bird, after all.

"And so you'll stay for a while?"

Regina was glad to turn from the window.

"If I may."

"Certainly, why not?" Marionette cackled. "God knows there's enough space. Why I have a house of this size, I don't know. Never see any of it except this room."

Regina was searching for a tactful rejoinder, when her eye fell on a photograph on the bedside table. It was in a silver frame; a young man, taken in profile. She caught her breath at the sheer beauty of him: he was the handsomest man she had ever seen. For the first time since Regina had entered the bedroom, Marionette turned her head away from her, following her eyes.

"Never touch that either." The voice was only a whisper, but it jarred as if someone had shouted. "Leave it be, or you'll regret it. Do you hear me?"

Regina opened her mouth to assure Marionette that she would never lay a finger on the photograph, when it happened.

Afterwards, she could not really remember the details of the occurrence, but at the time it was the most frightening thing which had ever befallen her. It was just as if the woman in the bed had caught her by the hands and was drawing her physically forward. The sensation only lasted a second or two, and then it was gone. The paralysed woman hadn't moved: she still sat stiffly against her pillows, fingers motionless. Louis was contemplating the carpet as before.

Regina swallowed hard.

"Yes, I understand."

She couldn't recall what else they talked about, answering questions mechanically until finally Marionette dismissed her and Louis as if they were mere servants.

Outside, Louis gave Regina a sorrowful look.

"I'm so sorry, my dear, truly sorry. I can see you're upset, but she isn't like other people, is she? I tried to tell you, but I didn't make a very good job of it. I ought to have made you understand, so that it wasn't such a shock to you. I should have been honest too, and told you that some of what is said about her is actually true. She is not as others are: Marionette isn't quite normal."

Regina was given a room in the back annexe, an unexpected excrescence at the rear of the building, five steps up from each of the main floors. It was comfortable and well-appointed, with primrose coloured wallpaper, curtains the shade of grass in summer-time, and a thick carpet which mingled the two hues in gentle harmony. The canopied bed was high and felt soft to her touch; the furniture best oak, inlaid with mother-of-pearl.

The housemaid who brought hot water and clean towels, announcing herself as Tottie May, took her time as she put a new piece of scented soap on the marble washstand, slyly taking in every detail of Regina's gown and the rope of real pearls round her slender neck. Tottie May was short and fat, with russet hair and queer yellowish eyes. She looked indolent, and not nearly as clean as Effie McGee, but she gave a friendly enough grin as she left Regina to dress for dinner.

When Regina reached the dining-room, Louis introduced her to the others, and soon they were seated round the oval table, meticulously set with a service of Coalport china, winking silver, and crystal glasses.

Effie served the meal, for the Boussards did not have a butler. Carrot soup à la Crécy; brill, with a piquant shrimp sauce; haunch of mutton spiced with capers; boiled ham dressed with brussel sprouts; soufflé of rice; ices, and an orange jelly.

"You have a good cook, uncle," said Regina, more to break the awkward silence than for any other reason. "This soufflé is quite excellent."

"Yes, Millie Butcher has been with us for some time." Louis had merely played with his food, totally unappreciative of its quality. "She started work as a scullerymaid when she was eight, I believe. She came here some seven years ago."

"Six."

Marcelle corrected him at once, overdressed in strident purple, spooning ice cream into her mouth like a glutton.

"Was it? I can't remember."

The brief exchange died again, and Regina stole another glance round the table. Victor, at eighteen, was very like his mother, with the same reddish hair and fresh complexion. He had paid Regina no attention at all, hardly acknowledging her existence when they had first met. He was only interested in Conrad Von Heltz, a good-looking German, and there was something about his concentration which made Regina feel unclean. She turned quickly to Jeanne instead.

Jeanne, the dumb sixteen-year-old, hardly raised her head throughout the meal. Her light brown hair was drawn severely back and tied with a dejected bow. It was as if Marcelle had chosen the most unattractive dress she could find in which to clothe her daughter, for the dull grey was far too old for the child and made her look sallow. Once, when she did look up, Regina saw that she had rather fine hazel eyes, but they were filled with a kind of mute fear.

At first, Regina was startled. Why should Jeanne be afraid? Then she remembered her own interview with Marionette, and gave an imperceptible shrug. No doubt Jeanne was frightened of Mme. Boussard, and little wonder. There couldn't be any other reason.

She tried again.

"I hear you are writing a book, Herr Von Heltz. That must be most interesting."

She was determined to break the oppression which hung over the table like a pall. It wasn't natural. Most families chatted at meal-times, if only to argue with one another.

"About old buildings, I think Uncle Louis said."

Von Heltz's gaze flickered in her direction, but she felt as though he were looking straight through her.

"Yes, that is correct." His voice was clipped, marked by a strong accent. "To-morrow I go to the Tower of London again. There is much more to see before I can write about it."

"I may go with you, Conrad, mayn't I?" Victor was suddenly animated, as if he had just come to life. "You'll let me go with you, won't you?"

"Of course, my dear boy, of course."

Regina felt the same spasm of unease somewhere in the back of her mind, thrusting it away determinedly as she switched her attention to Denys Pritchard, who was wiping his moustache carefully with his napkin. He was small, dapper and very neat in dress, with hair well plastered down with Macassar oil. It was hard to ignore the fact that he was common. As Louis had said, Marcelle had not made a good marriage. Denys had no breeding and no head for business either, a disastrous combination.

It was difficult to understand what the haughty Marcelle had seen in Denys, but, it was equally hard to find a reason for Pritchard's action in marrying Marcelle. They seemed poles apart, and Regina was wondering rather guiltily about their marriage bed, when Marcelle said:

"Are you going out to-night, Denys? I don't think you should. It's still snowing."

"I'll be all right, dear." Denys was folding the linen square very precisely. "It's Wagner to-night. Wouldn't want to miss that."

"Please yourself, although I think you're foolish to risk a chill." She turned to Regina. "My husband is very fond of music, you see. It's a positive mania with him. There's a small concert hall not far away, and I believe Denys would live there if he could."

Pritchard smiled politely at his wife's tart jest.

"It's true, Miss Curtis, I am fond of music. Nothing I like better than a good symphony."

The slightly nasal voice was common too, and the idea of Denys Pritchard as an ardent lover of music was as unlikely as the notion that Marionette possessed unaccountable powers.

Regina gave an inward curse. She had made herself a promise that she would not think about Marionette again that night. Soon, she would have to go to her room in the annexe, isolated and quite a long way away from the rest of the family. Such reflections would not make good night companions.

"Well, don't wake me up if you're late back." Marcelle helped herself to the largest piece of Turkish Delight in the bon-bon dish in front of her. "Use the dressing-room; I need my sleep. And, Jeanne! For goodness sake sit upright! You'll get round shouldered, slumped like that. How many more times do I have to tell you?"

An ugly red stained the girl's cheeks, the bent head remaining as it was. It was clear that Jeanne was used to such criticisms from her mother.

"What does it matter how she sits?" Victor was scornful. "Who's going to look at her?"

"Victor!"

Victor ignored Louis's protest.

"Well, it's true. She's as plain as a pike-staff; everyone says so."

"I don't." Regina said it very clearly, and gave the obnoxious Victor a hard look. "I think Jeanne is very pretty."

"Don't waste your sympathy on her," advised Marcelle as she popped another sweetmeat into her mouth. "She doesn't care what she looks like, nor what people think of her." She heaved a sigh. "Such a disappointment to me. I'd always hoped she'd take after me." She patted her hair, eyes dreamy. "Everyone said I was a beauty when I was Jeanne's age."

When there was no response, the pouting mouth grew sullen.

"I'm tired," she said shortly. "Effie, I'll have coffee in my room. Tell that idle girl, Rea, to bring it up to me, and make sure it's really hot."

With Marcelle's departure, the uncomfortable meal was over. Jeanne slipped away, and Von Heltz and Victor walked to the door together. They did not touch each other, yet it seemed to Regina as if they were holding hands.

In the sitting-room, Effie served coffee to Louis and Regina, and when the maid had gone, Boussard said:

"I expect you find them all rather different from what you had expected, don't you?"

"Yes, I suppose I do. One always pictures people in a certain way, and finds them to be completely the opposite. Poor Jeanne."

"Yes, that's very sad, and Victor is a bully. I suppose he'll grow out of it in time."

"His mother doesn't chide him for his unkindness."

"No, he's the apple of her eye, and she hasn't much time for her daughter, as you have seen."

"Why doesn't his father say something?"

Louis's lips moved fractionally.

"Denys? I think he's a bit afraid of Victor. Besides, Marcelle would never let him forget it if he upset her precious son."

It was on the tip of Regina's tongue to ask more about Von Heltz and his apparent affection for Victor, but something stopped her. It might embarrass Louis, and he looked troubled enough as it was. Instead, she changed the subject.

"Tell me more about Jules Marigny. Was he really as clever as people said?"

"Oh yes." Louis's eyes lit up, the sorrow and depression gone. "He was brilliant. To see him work the dolls was an experience never to be forgotten. Yes, he was a real master."

He coloured, looking rather shy.

"Do you know, after his death I began to make puppets myself."

"Did you?" Regina saw the happiness in his face, suspecting it to be a rare experience for him. "But how wonderful."

He laughed gently.

"Well, they weren't wonderful at first, I'm afraid. Rather crude, in fact, and made of any old bits of wood I could get hold of. I thought I should never learn to master the crutch, or control, either. But I persevered and went to see shows put on by experts, so that I could learn more. I even watched the street *fantoccini*. I was greedy for help, and not proud where I got it from. I mustn't boast, of course, but now I think my efforts are rather good. I used to give little shows in my wife's room to amuse her. She adored her father's dolls as much as he did. It was no coincidence that Jules named his first child Marionette." The amusement faded and his voice was heavy again. "Then ..."

"Yes?"

"Well, about two years ago she told me to take them out of the house. She said she never wanted to see them again. I don't know why. I didn't ask. It's better not to question her."

"You mean you stopped making puppets?"

"Oh no, I couldn't have done that!" The worried look vanished once more. "No, indeed, I didn't stop. In fact, in a way I have to be grateful to my wife, for when she sent me and my dolls packing, I did something I had meant to do for years, but had never got around to it. I turned the shed at the bottom of the garden into a workshop and theatre." He was like a small boy, eager and enthusiastic, looking years younger. "I've got real velvet curtains, and a proscenium, with a bridge, and plenty of room for the wood, tools and paints I need. I'll show you soon, if it won't bore you."

"You know it won't. I'd love to see the workshop. Uncle Louis."

"Yes?"

"Why did Aunt Marionette say I wasn't to touch her?" Regina

was making much of stirring her drink. "I only meant to kiss her."

"I know, I know." He was soothing. "You mustn't mind her, she's a sick woman. As to why she doesn't want to be touched, that's just because she was so badly hurt. Even I have never seen the extent of her injuries; she'd never shew me. Only Loveday Preece knows how maimed she was."

"How dreadful, and how stupid of me not to have realised what she meant. I'm so sorry; it was just that when she said it ... I ..."

"I know; it sounded rather frightening."

"Yes, in a way. How well you understand. You won't think me terribly inquisitive or insensitive, will you, but did Aunt Marionette get that scar in the accident?"

"I don't think you could ever be insensitive." He finished his beverage, savouring its strength. "As to the scar, well no, that wasn't caused by the accident."

He was holding back, and Regina could feel apprehension mounting inside herself.

"Don't tell me if you'd rather not."

"It's all right. There's no reason why you shouldn't know, although the truth of it isn't pretty." His face had lost its glow, drawn and weary as he stared down at his hands. "That happened some ten years back. Marionette said I wasn't paying enough attention to her; that I cared for my puppets more than I did for her. It wasn't true, of course, but that's what she thought. In those days I made them in my bedroom, because it was before I converted the shed. She said I spent all my time with them. One day when I went in to see her, she accused me of being in love with one of them. She had a pair of scissors in her hand. She'd been embroidering a tray-cloth. I can still remember it; it had sprays of lilac on it."

His head was bowed lower than ever, his voice laden with tears.

"Don't ... don't ... if you'd rather not."

He didn't seem to hear Regina, almost talking to himself.

"I sensed that something was wrong as soon as she spoke. There was real jealousy in her voice, and then I saw her hand move, but I couldn't get to her in time."

"Uncle!"

"Her cheek was torn open." He shook his head, eyes misty. "She used such violence, you see. And the blood; I've never seen so much. It covered the sheets and the tray-cloth until all the lilacs were gone."

He pulled himself together, seeing Regina's shocked face.

"Forgive me, my dear, I've upset you. I haven't spoken of it to anyone for years. I didn't realise it still hurt so much."

"I'm so sorry." Regina was near to tears too, not so much for Marionette as for Boussard. "I shouldn't have asked."

"It wasn't your fault; you weren't to know."

"It must have been awful."

"Yes, it was, although after that she wasn't jealous any more. She let me shew the puppets, as I've told you, and seemed to appreciate what I was doing, although ..."

Regina was afraid to ask, but she had to.

"Although what?"

He straightened up and met her compassionate gaze.

"Well, not only were her looks destroyed, but she was never quite the same after that day. From that time onwards, she changed. It was after that, that the whispers first began. My poor, poor love. That is when people first started to say that Marionette was a witch."

Regina was already in bed when Rea Hoole, the kitchenmaid, slid into the room with a cup of hot chocolate.

Rea was fourteen, with a pink button of a nose, bundled up in a frock several sizes too large for her.

"Tottie May sent me," she said, surreptitiously wiping her nose on her sleeve. "They be busy to-night, so I come." She put the cup down very carefully by the bed. "After this, we'll put your night drink on the table outside the door, likes we do for the others. Sometimes Tottie May does it, but mostly me. Tottie May don't like the stairs."

"Thank you, Rea."

Regina studied the pinched little face with concern. The child looked as if she wanted a good meal, her hands red and bleeding through constant immersion in hot water and the use of strong soap. She also looked as frightened as Jeanne had done, and Regina said casually:

"How long have you worked for my aunt?"

"Just a year, Miss." Rea was sidling away from the bed. "Come from the workhouse when me ma died."

"Do you like it here?"

The girl looked longingly at the door, obviously wishing she could evade Regina's questions.

"It's all right."

"It's a big place to keep clean." Regina was watching Rea over the rim of the cup. "You must have to work very hard."

"Don't mind that. It's just ..."

"Yes?"

"Nothin'."

"What don't you like?" Regina was soft and persuasive. "Is it because it's so quiet?"

She saw Rea twitch nervously.

"You noticed?"

"Yes, I did. It's difficult not to, isn't it? I expect you find it very different from the ..."

Rea gave an unchildlike laugh at Regina's hesitation.

"The House? Aye, it were noisy enough there, what with the drunkards and those what were mad. Then there are them birds."

"Birds?"

Regina saw Rea Hoole's colour recede. Birds in a workhouse?

"I don't understand," she said finally. "What kind of birds were there in the workhouse?"

It was Rea's turn to stare.

"Workhouse? Oh no, Miss, not there. The birds what are 'ere, I mean. The crows."

Regina put her cup down cautiously trying not to let it jangle on its saucer.

"I see. The crows."

They looked at one another silently. Then Regina said slowly:

"There was a crow on Mme. Boussard's window sill. I noticed it when I went to see her this afternoon."

"Yes, that's the only place they go. Don't see 'em anywhere else; just there. All weathers too. Yesterday there was two of 'em. That means a death."

"Oh come!"

"It's true." The girl was indignant at Regina's forced smile. "One for a warnin', two for a death. Someone will die, mark my words, and watch out for them dolls too."

Then she was gone, a timid wraith melting noiselessly away. Regina waited a full ten minutes before she could bring herself to blow out her candle. The thought of the blackness and the distance from the other bedrooms made her cling to the light, and Rea's words hadn't helped.

Then she sat up and snuffed the flame out defiantly. She was being utterly stupid. Rea was ignorant and superstitious, and Marionette an ill, and probably unstable, woman. There was no more to it than that, and nothing at all to be afraid of.

It was when she was at last growing sleepy that she heard it, propping herself up on one elbow straining her ears. It was a woman's voice, singing a strange, haunting tune. It made Regina's flesh creep, as if someone had walked over her grave.

She realised that she ought to overcome her cowardice and get up to investigate, but she couldn't do it. She knew she would never dare to open the door, never mind venture down the stairs to find out who it was.

As the singing died away, the silence took over again. Regina lay taut and on edge, listening for any sound which would assure her that she wasn't alone in the world. Even the squeak of a mouse would have been welcome just then.

Finally it came, the slam of a door somewhere far off, and Regina let her breath go. She wasn't alone, after all; there was at least one other person about.

With a thankful sigh she turned on her side and pulled the bedclothes well over her head, squeezing her lids tightly shut until sleep finally came and put an end to the fears.

Two

Much to her surprise, Regina's night passed peacefully. She slept well until seven-thirty, when she awoke in time to hear her morning tray being laid somewhat noisily on the table outside the door.

After breakfast, she sought Louis's permission to explore the house.

"Not the bedrooms, of course," she assured him hastily, "but I would love to look at the rest of it, especially the kitchen. I think a kitchen is the most satisfying room of all, don't you?"

Louis smiled vaguely.

"I've never really thought about it," he confessed. "I don't think I've been down there for years, but you go, my dear. By all means, look round the house, and after that we'll go to the workshop if you like."

"That would be splendid." Regina was in palest grey merino that day, the cuirasse bodice ending in a point in front which made her already slender waist seem a mere hand-span, a pearl and silver brooch at her throat. "I shall look forward to that."

When she reached her destination, the chattering stopped at once, the servants overawed by such an unexpected vision at ten o'clock in the morning. Regina looked round in delight. It was just as a kitchen should be, smelling of freshly baked bread and honey cake; spotlessly clean; the monster of a range newly blackened. She drank it all in quickly: the burnished copper pans, the teapots and trays, the stewpans, flour-boxes, bellows, jelly-moulds, and a hundred and one other things essential to a well-run kitchen.

The dresser was colourful with plates and cups in yellow, blue and white, a winter plant in a bronze pot flourishing at one end. Along the shelves were the fairings, the delight of every servant: crude little pottery figures in various poses and comic situations.

She moved over to the mantelpiece, admiring the big round clock, plain and with no nonsense about it, and the photographs in white wood frames. There was one of Loveday Preece, fierce and stolid, standing next to a woman with a beaky nose and glasses.

Then she turned to look at the staff and smiled.

"I'm sorry to disturb you," she said, "but I couldn't resist coming down. As I told my uncle, the kitchen is my favourite place."

The slight reserve melted at once, as Millie Butcher introduced herself. She was a tiny woman, about sixty, with snow-white hair, rosy cheeks and violet eyes.

"Bless you, Miss, and you're welcome. I'm Mrs Butcher. Effie, Rea and Tottie May you've met already, of course, and this is Caleb Dummer. He's our gardener and handyman. Come in for a cuppa tea, for it's reel crool outside to-day. Mistress don't know 'e does that, but I'm sure you'll not say nothin'."

"No, of course, I won't." Regina was quick to promise. "Good-morning Dummer."

Caleb got to his feet with obvious reluctance. A big brawny man, strong as a bull, with a thatch of brown hair, greenish eyes and a heavy nose and chin. He looked sullen, yet Regina could see why Effie was ogling him. He had a certain animal attraction; vibrant and very much alive under the unfriendly surface.

"I'd like a cup too, if I may." Regina sat herself down in one of the rocking chairs by the fire. "I know I ought to wait for coffee upstairs and leave you in peace, but it's so warm and cosy down here."

"'Course you can 'ave one." Millie beamed at the praise of her domain. "Tottie May, get one of them best cups orf the dresser. A bit of cherry cake to go with it, Miss?"

Regina laughed, unaware that Dummer was watching the line of her throat and swell of her breasts with the eye of an expert.

"Good heavens no, Mrs Butcher! After what you prepared for my breakfast? I've not tasted egg and bacon like that for years."

The cook's face crinkled with pleasure.

"Well, don't suppose they 'ave such things in Paris, do they? I've 'eard they only eat them airy-fairy rolls. No way to start a day in my opinion."

The tea came, and a few more compliments were exchanged. Then Regina got down to business. She was cautious, for she didn't want to make them wary.

"Did anyone hear singing last night?" she asked off-handedly. "It was quite late; I was almost asleep when I heard it. A woman's voice, deep and sad."

She watched the servants exchange uneasy glances. Only Dummer seemed unmoved, cramming bread and dripping into his mouth with total unconcern.

Finally Mrs Butcher said:

"Best not to mention such things. Wiser to leave it be."

"But I can't. I want to know who it was. Surely there is no harm in that? Was it Mme. Boussard, or Mrs Pritchard?"

"No, it weren't them, nor Miss Jeanne neither."

"Then who?"

"Tell her, why don't you?" Caleb took a long swallow of scalding tea and wiped his sleeve across his lips. He'd never been so close to a real beauty before. Just like a painting he'd seen once; the same exquisite skin and silky hair. She looked a cool customer, but she might be quite different in bed; most women were. He cleared his throat. She weren't for the likes of him, more's the pity. "She'll not be satisfied until you do, and why keep it secret?"

"Keep what a secret?" Regina was watching the fear on the women's faces, not liking it. "I don't understand. What is it?"

There was another pause. Then Millie said quietly:

"Well, we 'ave 'eard singin' in the last week or so, it's true. No one knows what's doin' it, but we 'ears it."

"Mostly late at night," confirmed Tottie May, chopping away at some suet on the well-scrubbed table. "'Orrible, I calls it."

"But surely ..."

"It's a sign that more bad things are going to 'appen."

"Rea!"

There was a chorus of disapproval, and Rea turned scarlet.

"Don't be cross with her." Regina was very calm. "I did ask, you know. What sort of things do you mean?"

"Get that cake out o' the oven." Millie was still irritated with Rea. "Be burnt to a cinder. Do somethin' useful, 'stead of frightening Miss Curtis."

"I'm not afraid," said Regina untruthfully. "Do tell me. What sort of things do you mean?"

Dummer gave a short laugh.

"You'd be surprised, and that's a fact. Can't think why any of 'em stay 'ere."

The cake was turned carefully on to a tray, golden brown, smelling deliciously of hot cinnamon.

"That looks lovely, Mrs Butcher. How clever you are. I wish I could cook like that. Why do you stay if you're nervous?"

Millie's lips were compressed.

"Good enough place, this. Got a room of me own: small, but me own. Last job I 'ad, I shared a bed with the 'ousemaid, and she was a dirty slut. Put up with a lot to be on me own, I would. Then there's the wages, what are good, and missus don't bother with 'ow much we eat. Don't even 'ave to find our own tea and sugar, like most."

"But you all say you see things." Caleb was leering at Millie, riling her. "What good's tea and sugar when you're scared stiff?"

"I'm not scared, Caleb Dummer, and mind yer lip, or you'll get nothing' more in this 'ere kitchen. Whatever will Miss Curtis think of us?"

Regina met the cook's almost pathetic anxiety, and said softly:

"Don't worry, Mrs Butcher. There is something wrong with this house. I felt it as soon as I came into it. I won't breathe a word, but tell me what happens. Why are you frightened, and who is the woman who sings at night?"

"That we reelly don't know, Miss, honest. Like Mrs B. says, we've only 'eard it recently." Effie was twisting the strings of her apron, her attention diverted from Caleb for the moment. "But things did ... did 'appen before that. Like Floss Baker, what fell down the stairs to the wood cellar and broke 'er neck.''

Regina's lips parted, but she didn't snap the thread by an interruption.

"And then there was those two companions. Olive Booth and Dora Jones. Both of 'em vanished, and not a soul knows the goin' of 'em.''

"Vanished?''

"That's right." Caleb grinned savagely. He could see the alarm in the silver-haired girl, and it was like balm to his soul. Maybe he could never possess her, but he could put the fear of God into her. "'Ere one minute, gone the next. Never seen no more, neither of 'em.''

"Get back ter yer work, Caleb," said Millie snappily. "We've 'ad enough o' you for one mornin'. Anyone 'ud think you'd got nothin' to do.''

They watched him slouch off, slamming the door behind him.

"Take no notice of 'im." Mrs Butcher was trying to repair the damage. "Likes to tease us, 'e does. Thinks it's funny.''

"But you are worried, aren't you?" Regina was gentle. "Is it true what he said? Did two of Mme. Boussard's companions disappear?''

"Well, they did go rather sudden like." Mrs Butcher was beating eggs with unnecessary force. "Reel puzzle, it was, both goin' the same way.''

"And all of 'em 'ad upset 'er." Rea had recovered slightly, risking another reprimand. "Floss broke missus's favourite cup the afternoon afore she fell down them stairs. Miss Booth and Miss Jones 'ad 'ad words with 'er too. She said they'd be punished: Loveday Preece told us that. And they was, wasn't they?''

"But that must have been a coincidence." Regina did not sound convinced, even to herself. "You can't really believe ...''

"Can't say we do, can't say we don't." Millie motioned the scullerymaid to be quiet. "But it's just as the girl says. They'd all upset 'er one way or another.''

"She's a witch." Rea blurted it out, ignoring cook's glare.

"Everyone knows that. Didn't you see the willows in the vase in 'er room? Witches worship the willow. My ma told me that."

"I'll box your ears for you if you don't keep that clatterin' tongue of yours still." Mrs Butcher thumped the flour-shaker down and picked up a spoon. "Never known such a wench for spreadin' silly tales as this one. Wants 'er bottom tanned, that's what she wants."

"It's true!" Rea was defiant, braving the thought of a beating. "And what about the crows? I told you, Miss, they come to warn. Don't never drive 'em off, will you? They don't belong to 'er, of course. They just come to tell 'er of the future. Now they've come to tell 'er of a death. And that's not all. Likes I told you last night, watch out for them dolls. They don't want to stay in that shed. They want the 'ouse, and in the end they'll get it."

Mrs Butcher abandoned the spoon and caught Rea by the arm, giving her a good shake.

"One more word out of you, you slut, and you'll get a right walloping. 'Old yer peace, will you? Do you want to get us all put out on the streets?"

"I shall say nothing." Regina was very thoughtful. "I gave my promise. I think Rea is wrong about my aunt, but someone was singing, and the house is not like any other I've known."

"That's 'cos it's possessed." Effie was mumbling, as fearful of Mrs Butcher as she was of No: 7, Chantry Close. "We all knows it, but, like Mrs B. says, it's a good position. Places like this is 'ard to find. We puts up with it, you see. Ain't 'urt us so far."

Millie released Rea and went back to her work.

"You goin' 'ome soon, Miss?" she asked as she began to mix the flour and eggs together. "Not stayin' long, are you?"

"Not long. Why?"

"Well, best to be on the safe side, I always say. No need to take risks unless you've got to. You go 'ome as soon as you can. Don't 'old with all that this stupid chit says, but she's right about one thing. Mistress is a right odd one, beggin' your pardon, Miss, seein' she's your aunt. But the last time those dratted crows came, Dora Jones went out very early next mornin' and never came back."

Regina walked through the garden with Louis Boussard, shaking under her brown paletot trimmed with beaver. It wasn't just the icy ground, or the shrill cut of the wind which made her quake. It was her conversation with the servants. She told herself not to be such a ninny. Servants' gossip was never reliable, for they were easily bored and always delighted to have some excitement in their drab lives. Yet they had looked genuinely frightened. Even the ebullient little cook had been nervous. She tried to put the disquiet aside as Louis unlocked the door of the shed.

It was a sturdy building, almost invisible from the house, hidden by trees. Inside it was dark until oil-lamps were lit, and then Regina could see the neatly kept benches and the shelves stacked with paints and wood and bales of expensive materials.

At one end there was the promised proscenium, green velvet curtains closed: at the other, a huge mirror almost covering the wall.

"I need that to watch the dolls," explained Louis, busy with a lantern. "I have to lean over the bridge which is behind the curtains, and work the marionettes from above. I can't really see the true effect, except in the glass."

"No, of course not; I hadn't thought of that. What lovely materials."

He chuckled.

"Oh yes, my babies are very well-dressed. I'm lucky too to have found a woman to make the costumes for me, for I'm no good with a needle. Her name is Eda Trott, poor soul. I'm afraid her husband is a brute; always beating her. I let her sleep here when she wants to, just to get away from him for a while."

"How kind you are." Regina was looking at the sharp chisels on the bench. "It must take a long time to make each marionette."

"Some take several weeks; others I can do quite quickly. I make their faces of wax or pâpier-maché, and every one of them has real glass eyes and human hair. Jules Marigny insisted that realism was everything, you know."

"Is it an old craft?"

"Indeed it is. The ancient Greeks called puppets *neurospasta*, and in later centuries they still held their own. There was a remarkable puppet opera in Paris in 1674, and in the seventeen hundreds there were such shows as Powell's Puppet Show, Pinkethman's, Charlotte Clarke's, near the Haymarket, and Flocton's, which had five hundred marionettes, all working. No, there's nothing new about the dolls."

They moved on, Regina grimacing as they passed a table covered with pieces of hair of various shades. It was as if a whole army of tiny people had been scalped to supply M. Boussard with his needs. They stopped again for Louis to shew Regina how he joined the body to the limbs with screw-eyes and wire pins, sighing a little as he confessed that the fixing made a slight clicking noise as the puppets moved.

"I still haven't quite overcome that problem, but I will in time."

Regina nodded, the smell of the glue kettle making her want to sneeze.

Finally, they made their way up the steps beside the proscenium, and a second later she saw them. Now, there was only the single lamp in Louis's hand to illuminate the scene, and as the marionettes came into view, Regina went cold all over.

They hung limply on their hooks, as if someone had deprived them temporarily of motion, yet they were so incredibly real that she almost drew back. Most were about two foot in height, the gleam of the lamp catching the glass orbs and making them shine with terrible intelligence. Rea's words came back to her with a rush. They didn't want to stay in the shed: they wanted to take over the house.

"It has to be remembered," said Louis, apparently unaware of Regina's reaction, "that one sees a puppet from some way away. As you will notice, there are some benches down there. Now and then the family and servants come to see my show. Although Jules, and most famous exponents of *fantoccini*, hold that realism is vital, as I told you, I have often wondered whether there are not experiments which could be made, bearing in mind the distance between the doll and the audience. See, like this one."

He reached up and took a puppet from its peg. It was a

dancing girl, with hollowed sockets painted pale green in place of eyes, dressed in flounces and lace.

"There, you see. It may look unreal now, but from ten feet away, it would be quite different. More subtle, don't you think?"

Regina gulped. It was almost worse than the conversation in the kitchen, but she forced herself to be rational. They were only pieces of wood joined together, clad in scraps of silk and satin, yet even the blind sockets seemed to be watching her with peculiar intensity.

"Yes, I'm sure you're right. Oh!"

Louis turned a benign gaze on her.

"What is it?"

"That doll over there; the one in black, with the sharp nose and glasses. It reminds me of someone, but I can't think who." Regina stared at it for a moment longer, then said slowly: "Oh yes, I know. It's the woman in the photograph on the mantelpiece in the kitchen."

Louis laughed and patted her arm.

"Very observant, and a compliment to me. I haven't seen the photograph because, as I told you, I don't go down to the kitchen, but I know the servants are always having them taken, goodness knows why. This one is a likeness of a companion of Marionette's; Olive Booth. I like to make models of those who have served my dearest so well. A small 'thank you', as it were. I've made models of everyone in the house, as a matter of fact. I'll make one of you too, to add to my collection. You are so lovely, and it will be a reminder of you when you return to Paris."

"What happened to Olive Booth?"

He hung the dancer back on her hook, shrugging his shoulders.

"No one knows. I saw her go out about six o'clock one morning, but she didn't return. I suppose she found Marionette too much for her, like Dora Jones did. Later, we found that their things had all gone. They must have moved their boxes and possessions some time before."

"Miss Jones went too?"

"Yes, just like Miss Booth. I noticed her by the gate. I thought she was going for a walk. I remember thinking she looked ill; very pale, you know." He raised his hands helplessly. "We didn't try to replace them. After all, Loveday always did most of what was required. The other women just ran small errands or read to your aunt, and did a bit of sewing."

"But didn't you try to find out what had happened to them?"

"Why no." Boussard looked surprised. "There was no reason for that. They'd gone of their own free will, and I knew why. It was because of Marionette, and what was said of her, that scared them off. Poor dears; I don't know how they'd get another position without a reference."

He stretched up and took down another puppet. This time it was a clown, gay and bright in a baggy suit with brilliant patches. Its face was the colour of chalk, lips scarlet and hideously wide. As it swung round on its strings, the glass eyes seemed to be looking straight at Regina, as if it could really see her.

She watched as Louis worked the controls, gasping at its antics as it gambolled about in the half-light. It was no longer a marionette, but a miniature circus performer.

"That is unbelievable! It's just as if it were ... were alive."

Louis's smile was shy.

"Thank you. I don't often get praise, but I'm weak enough to enjoy it when it does come."

He let the clown do another somersault or two, and then put it away. At once life was gone: it was just a few pieces of satin and spangles, hanging slackly against the back screen, and Regina's pulse slowed down to normal.

"My ambition has always been to make a full-size marionette," said Louis as they made their way to the door. "And now I've thought of a way of doing it. As soon as it's ready, you shall see it. I couldn't make it of wood, of course, for that would have been too heavy, but I've found the answer at last, and I'm really excited about it."

"I shall look forward to seeing it." Regina's response was flat as they stepped out into the frosty air, for the awesome spell which Louis's other family had cast over her had not quite faded. "I went to the kitchen earlier this morning."

"Yes, you told me. Where you saw Olive's photograph. And did everything come up to expectations?" Boussard was locking the shed. "I hope you weren't disappointed."

"No, it was just as I imagined it would be." She had promised cook and the others not to repeat what they had said, and so she crossed her fingers behind her back and lied boldly. "I saw the iron stairs which led down to the lower level too. They looked quite dangerous."

M. Boussard wrapped his scarf tighter about his throat, head bent to the wind.

"They are, I'm afraid. There was an accident a few years ago. A maid, I think her name was Floss, went down one evening to get some logs. She tripped and fell. Broke her neck. I ought to do something about them, but somehow there never seems to be the time."

"Uncle, forgive me if I'm asking too many questions, but those two companions. Had they had words with Aunt Marionette? I mean, did they argue with her, or displease her in some way, or did they just go for no reason at all?"

"What a gale!" Louis was fighting against the rough gust which hit them. "Arguments? I don't think so. Not that I heard of, anyway. Of course, it's easy enough to get on the wrong side of your aunt, for the sick are always fractious. Usually, though, the companions she's had have been good-tempered and long-suffering. They have to be, you know, to earn their living. No, it's as I said. They were frightened off by the gossiping."

There was nothing more Regina could say. To press the subject would be to create suspicion. Besides, it was obvious that Louis knew nothing more than the fact that the two women had run away. To him, the logical explanation was that they couldn't stand Marionette and her reputation any longer. He accepted it without question and hadn't tried to find them.

"Thank you for shewing me your theatre," she said when they were back in the warmth again. "I thought it quite fascinating."

He nodded, smiling gently.

"And a bit unnerving?"

She coloured, and he chuckled.

"Don't worry, I won't tell anyone. It was just that I saw your face when you were looking at my darlings. It's natural enough. Until one gets used to them, they can be a bit scary. I'll put on a show for you before you leave, so that you can get to know them properly."

Effie had appeared and taken his coat and scarf, and when he had gone off to the study, rubbing his hands to bring them back to life, she said dubiously:

"Saw them, did you?"

"Yes." Regina was reserved, still put out of countenance by the fact that Louis had noticed her fear. "Yes, I did. M. Boussard is very gifted."

"Maybe, but they're 'eathen things. We all 'ates goin' to see 'em, but we daresn't refuse. Don't do to offend Master, you understand. Did you see 'em all?"

"No, not really." Regina wished Effie would go away. "But I did see one which looked like the woman in the photograph in the kitchen."

Effie's lips twisted.

"Miss Booth? Aye, 'e made a likeness of 'er, but then 'e's made one of us all, even me. Gawd, it gave me a right turn when I saw it, for there was no mistakin' 'oo it was meant to be. Rea says the dolls borrow the souls of those what they look like, and come to life. Don't think it's true, do you?"

"No, of course not." Regina forced herself to be reassuring as she made for the stairs. "That's just Rea and her fanciful ideas."

But as she went up the first flight, damp kid boots sinking deep into thick pile, she felt a quick pang of worry. Not only had Rea said the dolls borrowed the souls of those whom they represented, and Louis Boussard had just promised to make one in her image, but the kitchenmaid had spoken of the marionettes as if they were living things. Tired of the shed, she had said; waiting to vacate it for better quarters.

It wasn't a nice thought, and her heart was thumping hard as she went into her room and closed the door hastily behind her.

That night, Marcelle and Denys Pritchard were dressing for

dinner. Denys was in the slip-room, humming to himself, whilst Marcelle considered her reflection in the mirror.

She had touched her face with powder, her lips with a trace of carmine. Good enough natural colour in the cheeks: no need for rouge. She raised one hand, fluffing out her fringe, cocking her head to admire the new dress of emerald green. It had been expensive: off the shoulder, and trimmed lavishly with embroidery, but it was worth it. Her shoulders and breasts were still her best feature: thick, flawless skin, pure white. She was proud of them, and she knew that he admired them too. She'd seen the look in his eyes on previous occasions when he had studied the firm flesh, and it had aroused a hot and instant desire in her.

Thank God Denys was going out that night. She scorned him as a namby-pamby, with his stupid pretence about concerts. No go in him at all, and hopeless as a husband, but at least he made himself scarce most of the time.

Of course, if anyone knew what she did some nights when Denys was gone, they would have been shocked. They wouldn't expect her to let another man take her, but who cared what they thought? It was like living in a mausoleum in Marionette's house. Her cousin wouldn't even let her furnish the bedroom which she and Denys shared in the way she wanted to. Sometimes she'd even considered running away, but there was nowhere to go. If Denys hadn't been so feeble, they wouldn't have had to spend the last seven years here. After his last venture had failed dismally, there'd been no choice but to turn to Marionette.

Marionette had the money, making a grudging but sufficient allowance to her cousin and her family, but only for as long as they lived under her roof. She liked to control them; to tell them when they should eat; when she expected them to retire for the night; which service to attend at church on Sundays. They were virtually prisoners, frowned upon if so much as a vase was moved out of its rightful place. Loveday Preece's beady eyes were everywhere, and her reports to her mistress were thorough.

Marcelle bared her teeth as she fastened a rope of artificial pearls round her neck. She hated Marionette. Her cousin was a spiteful cat, invalid or not. A loathsome woman who loved power, but there was nothing which could be done about it until she died, and surely that couldn't be much longer. She knew what the half-witted servants said about their mistress, but she scoffed them to scorn. A witch indeed! Bitch, perhaps, but nothing more.

She pushed Marionette out of her mind and thought about him again, her small eyes closing in bliss. Just remembering him made her tremble. When they were together, she was putty in his hands, and she would take anything from him, even the humiliation of being told now and then that he had other things to do. Only a month ago, he'd come to the side door, her smile fading when he told her to go to bed. She'd pleaded with him, swallowing her pride, but he'd walked away. She'd been so angry at the time that when she saw the other man slouch up to her, she hadn't slammed the door in his face. She hadn't even drawn back when his hand touched her bare shoulder.

He hadn't been like her true love, of course, but he'd satisfied her at the time. Strong and powerful, renewing her self-confidence as he assuaged her hunger.

She rose, picking up her fan.

"Are you ready, Denys?" She was shrill, her dreaming over. "It's nearly eight."

"Almost, my duck."

"I wish you wouldn't call me that."

"What?"

"That! My duck. It's so vulgar. Denys, do hurry up!"

Pritchard patted strong-smelling lotion on his cheeks and gave his hair a final brush.

He wished Marcelle would stop shouting. Her raucous voice hammered on his nerves, but soon the meal would be over and he'd be able to get away. He had had no qualms about marrying Marcelle, for when she was young she'd been slim and shapely, and there had been the aura of money about her.

But how he'd paid for it! He'd done his best, but she was insatiable; like a bitch on heat at night, pretending to be shocked by the mere allusion to sex by day. She'd robbed him of his confidence and his manhood as she mocked his failure in bed. The more he tried, the worse it became, and he hated her as much as she despised him. She was mean too. Every penny he needed had to be coaxed out of her with flattery, which she loved, and kisses which made him almost sick to bestow on her flabby cheeks. Luckily, he'd found that he was quite a successful gambler, and a game or two of cards now and then, when the others thought he was listening to Beethoven, had helped to provide the money he needed for his other life. The life he really cared about.

He smoothed his moustache carefully, pretending not to hear Marcelle screaming at him once more to make haste.

God Almighty, what a shrew! And as for her brats. One dumb and stupid, the other in love with a German sodomite. To think that they were his too; it was hard to believe. He'd often wished that he could have knocked Victor flat on his back for his insolence, but he'd never dared to try. Victor was not only too big; he enjoyed inflicting pain. Denys had found that out late one night, when he'd seen his son with one of the maids. Not content with pinching her bottom like any normal man, Victor had been twisting the girl's arm behind her back and lapping up the agony on her face. Bloody pervert. Pity he didn't fall downstairs as that maid had done some years before, or take himself off like those two drudges who'd had the sense to run away from their slavery.

He felt sorry in his heart for Louis Boussard. Fancy being married to that freak of a woman. It was almost worse than having to get into bed with Marcelle and try to satisfy her. At least Marcelle was whole, and no one had hinted that she could do peculiar things.

He paused, seeing his face a shade paler in the mirror.

Queer that; the things which were said about Marionette. Must be a lot of poppycock. After all, what could she do, stuck up there in her room, with half her body missing?

"Denys! Will you hurry up!"

He thrust the nervy thought away, almost glad for once to hear his wife's loud but reassuring bellow, flicking an eye over her as he came out of the dressing-room. She was hot for it again;

he could tell at once. He always knew by the kind of dress she wore, and that special perfume she used. Well, thank Christ it wasn't him she wanted. That at least was a relief.

"I'm ready, my duck," he said mildly. "Shall we go down?"

While her mother was preening herself in the mirror on the floor below, Jeanne was also preparing for dinner.

No paint or powder for her. Even if she had been allowed to use such things, she wouldn't have touched them. She thought her mother looked grotesque in the evenings, just like Uncle Louis's puppets which Jeanne feared so much.

Because she was regarded as a child, and thus of no importance, Jeanne had to make do with cold water, but she didn't care. As long as it was clean and pure; that was all that mattered. She poured the contents of the painted jug into a chipped basin and began to undress.

Ever since Victor, for whom she nursed a hatred almost as deep as that for her mother, had pushed her into the mud and held her there, she had felt unclean. Only six at the time, she had been terror-stricken, her mouth too full of ooze to scream, certain that she was going to die. She still remembered that afternoon with terrible clarity; a cold winter's day, with sullen skies and slush underfoot.

It was she, Jeanne, who had got the beating for getting her clothes dirty. Victor, his mother's darling, had merely smirked as he watched the strap applied to her small pink bottom.

Since then, Jeanne had become fanatical about cleanliness. At least three times a day she would strip and wash herself all over, just as if the mud was still sticking to her. She could feel the goose-pimples as she splashed herself with the icy water, but that wasn't important.

She wished she didn't have to go downstairs to the dining-room. She dreaded sitting at the table, glancing furtively at her companions when she thought they weren't looking, wondering which of them was going to die. She knew someone would die, for she'd heard the servants say so. Rea, for whom she felt pity and a certain affinity, since they were much alike despite the difference in their stations, had said the crows had come. Two crows for a death.

She rubbed herself vigorously with a towel, her hand suddenly stilled as a dreadful thought struck her. Perhaps it was she herself who would die. She was no more immune to death than anyone else, and if someone had found out about her secret, then she was in great danger.

Shaken, she stared at herself in the long oval mirror in the corner, critically and distastefully. Creamy skin, small budding breasts, slender hips, sloping shoulders and gently rounded arms. She hated her body, wishing she had been a boy. If she were a boy, she would be safe.

She was too engrossed in her thoughts to look round, and even if she had done so, it was doubtful whether she would have noticed the small knot hole just below the picture of Jesus in the Temple. Jeanne was hardly ever aware of her immediate surroundings: she was just conscious of a general feeling of dread in Aunt Marionette's spacious house.

A single bright eye moved behind the tiny gap, watching as Jeanne bent down to pick up her shift, unwinking and absorbed until the girl was fully clothed again. Then it was gone, the hole black and empty once more as Jeanne opened the door and braced herself to face the family.

Conrad Von Heltz and Victor were in the sitting-room, waiting for the dinner-gong to sound. It was a more private place at that time of day, for the others would either be coming downstairs, or assembling in the drawing-room.

They sat together on a couch, close, yet not touching each other.

"I'll have to go home next week, unless I have money." Conrad was studying Victor's stricken face. I don't want to go, you know that, but what can I do? I cannot stay in London penniless."

"I know." Victor managed to get the words out, his eyes moist with unshed tears. He'd never met anyone like Conrad before. So strong and handsome and sympathetic. Von Heltz had revealed a world to him he had never dreamed of. He couldn't let him go. "I'll get you some."

He made the promise boldly, not having the least idea how he would achieve his object, but determined to hold on to his idol.

"Your allowance is so small." Conrad's mouth curved sorrowfully. "Dear Victor, it wouldn't be enough."

"I'm not talking about my allowance." Victor cleared his throat. Conrad's voice was like a heady wine, making him drunk with an emotion he still did not quite understand. "I'll get proper money. I've given you my word. Please say that you won't go."

"Well ..." One strong, well-shaped hand covered Victor's. "I don't want to go, as I've said, and if we could overcome the financial problem, then ..."

"We will! We will!"

"Then I shall stay." The hand tightened. "How tiresome it is that people like you and I have to worry about such sordid things, but, alas, we cannot live without funds, can we?"

"No." Victor's lips were hard. "Marionette's got plenty, the old hag. She could give me some and never miss it, but she won't. Mother's got a bit tucked away too. She thinks no one guesses, but I know where it is. God, how I hate women! Painted harlots, the whole lot of them, and quite useless. They're disgusting the way they primp themselves, shewing off their ankles, trying to catch their prey."

"Mm."

Von Heltz's tone was still low and casual, but there was a glint in his eyes, business-like as he said smoothly:

"And you think you can persuade your mother to give you some money?"

"One way or the other."

They looked at each other for a long while. Then Von Heltz sighed.

"I won't ask you how." His smile was like a kiss. "I'll leave it all to you. Such a clever boy. No one appreciates you as I do."

"Oh Conrad!"

"Dearest Victor. Ah, the gong I think. Alas, we must join the others, but perhaps later we could meet to ... to discuss my book?"

"Yes, yes, later."

They moved to the door, hands by their sides again, talking of the inclement weather as they took their seats round the table and waited for Effie to serve the soup.

At ten-thirty that night, Rea began to scream.

Doors opened; startled heads poked out; hurried steps brought others down from the upper floors. Gathered round the terrified maid, it was Regina who spoke first.

"Rea! What is it? What's wrong?"

The screams had turned into gasping sobs, the girl apparently deaf to the question.

"Be quiet!" Marcelle's loud boom cut through the tears and silenced Rea instantly. "How dare you make such a commotion at this time of night. What's the matter with you?"

Rea glanced round the circle of faces. M. Boussard, wearing old grey flannel and looking gaunt; Herr Von Heltz, in a pure silk dressing-gown, with Victor at his elbow; Mrs Pritchard, strangely washed-out, devoid of her lip rouge and the Chinese ink and rosewater she painted on her eyebrows and lashes; Mr Pritchard, neat as ever, and not yet out of his top coat; Jeanne, cringing on the outskirts of the group, face as wan as Rea's own; Mrs Butcher, Effie and Tottie-May startled and half-asleep.

"I ... I ..."

."Get on with it," snapped Marcelle impatiently. "You've got a tongue in your head, haven't you? What made you shriek out like that and frighten us half to death?"

"I ... it was when I took madame's chocolate in." Rea was almost as scared of Mrs Pritchard as she was of Mme. Boussard, but in a different way. Mrs Pritchard was quick to use her hand, giving a clump to the head which made it ring or issuing peremptory orders to cook that Rea was not to have any supper, because she hadn't done her work properly. "I took the cup in, likes I often do, and then ..."

"And then what?"

Rea stole a quick look at Marcelle's thunderous face.

"Go on." Regina was quiet and without anger. "Tell us what happened."

Rea turned to her in relief. Miss Regina wouldn't shout at her, nor punish her for something which wasn't her fault.

"It was on the bedside table."

"What was? Is my aunt all right?"

"Oh yes, she's all right." The girl was ashen, thinking back to the moment when she had crossed to her mistress's bed. "She was sleepin', and she didn't stir, but on the table there was an eye. It stared at me somethin' awful."

"An eye! You must have been mistaken." Regina was shaken, but she gave no sign of it. "You must have imagined it."

"There was an eye." Rea was emphatic, red with frustration because everyone was watching her blotchy face in disbelief. "There was, I tells you. There was!"

Into the silence which followed, there came a snigger, and they all turned to look at Loveday Preece, who had come down from her attic bedroom to join them.

"Do you know anything about this?" demanded Marcelle, her normally rosy colour drained away. "What's the girl talking about? There couldn't have been an eye on the table. It's utter nonsense."

"Oh no it isn't." Loveday was sly. "She's right. Waking or sleeping, madame sees everything. Never think otherwise. I'll go to her. Tell her I'll watch for a while so she can rest proper. Best you all do the same."

They looked after her retreating form, hearing the titter of laughter as Loveday's candle danced along the corridor like a Will-o'-the-Wisp, and then vanished as she closed Marionette's door behind her.

Three

On the following night, Denys Pritchard was in the front parlour of No: 4, Kettle Street, Lambeth. It was a snug little room, crowded with knick-knacks and photographs, crammed with inexpensive furniture, and boasting a new carpet of bright reds and greens.

It was a far cry from Marionette Boussard's elegant home, but Denys sighed in contentment as he stretched his feet towards the blazing coal fire and watched Noreen Rutter bending down to undo his bootlaces.

She was a pretty woman of about twenty-five, with hair too tightly crimped, and wearing a rather vulgar Dolly Varden dress, the short overskirt bunched out behind like a giant puff of yellow silk. Not real silk, of course, for he hadn't been able to give Noreen that much money, yet she looked a real treat in spite of it. None of your hoity-toity airs about her, and more than accommodating in bed. Although he considered himself several cuts above her in the social scale, he always made a point of requesting her favours, not demanding them. It was not entirely a matter of humility: he was also afraid that too much arrogance might put her off him.

Noreen deserved a reward for the pleasure she gave him. Perhaps a necklace or some ear-rings. Now that he'd discovered where Marcelle hid her money, he might be able to do something about it. Maybe a pair of stockings for Noreen's delectable legs.

"There!" Noreen rose, Denys's slippers in place. "Come on, luv, your supper's ready. Got a nice bit of fish, and meat pie to follow, with some o' that cheese you're forever goin' on about."

She wasn't critical, laughing with him as she led him to the table and gave him a smacking kiss on his lips. He liked that. Noreen was never afraid of shewing her affection: not like Marcelle, who pretended she hated the touch of his hand, although he knew perfectly well that she craved for sexual satisfaction as much as he did. Noreen was different. Like a child in some ways; very much like a woman in others.

He drank his stout and tucked into the pie, smothering it in brown sauce. He enjoyed the coarser fare which Noreeen provided; something for a man to get his teeth into. He'd eaten at eight, but now it was after eleven, and he was ready for another bite. He'd always had a good appetite.

"How's things?" asked Noreen finally, when he had finished, and they were back by the fire again. "Anything new?"

"No, my chicken." He ruffled her hair affectionately. Soon they'd go into the bedroom which was up a narrow flight of stairs, just for an hour before he had to get back to Balham. "All about the same. That girl's still there; Marionette's niece. I told you about her. So's the bloody German." His face darkened. "Can't think what old Boussard is up to, letting a man like that stay in the house, and to think that my own son ..."

"There, there, pet." Noreen was soothing, drawing the anger from his face as she began to undo the top buttons of her bodice. "Don't think about them now. This is our time. Oh, Denys, I wish we could be together always."

His eyes were on her skin, smooth like alabaster.

"God, so do I." His voice thickened. "You're lovely, poppet, d'yer know that?"

"I'm glad you think so." She was discarding her stays now, freeing her body for him. "Maybe soon you'll be able to do what we talked about. Then we could be together."

"Aye, maybe soon. If we did manage it ..." He gave a deep sigh. "Well, if we did, we'd be together that's for sure. Well, no use crying for the moon yet. Our time'll come."

"Not too long, Denys." Noreen's brown eyes were melting

into his, but there was a definite firmness under her words. "Wouldn't want to wait till I was old."

"Won't be long." He was mumbling, mouth loose as he saw the chemise drop to her waist. "I promise, love, it won't be that long. Now come on; let's get to bed."

Next morning another visitor arrived at No: 7, Chantry Close. Regina came downstairs at ten-fifteen to find Louis talking animatedly to someone in the hall. At first, she could only see the newcomer's back, elegantly clad.

"Regina!" Louis held out his hand to her. "Another marvellous surprise! First you, and now Philippe. Come and meet him. This is Philippe Lavisse, the son of Marionette's cousin, René."

Regina came down the last few steps as Lavisse turned, and she caught her breath. It was as though someone had clutched at her heart and squeezed it hard, but the feeling was soon crushed beneath her formal greeting to the man who raised her hand to his lips with cool indifference.

Lavisse was tall and lean, with black hair curled slightly round a well-modelled head. His eyes were dark grey under heavy lids and thin eyebrows, cheekbones perfectly moulded to balance the firm chin and hard mouth. Regina, trying not to stare, was reminded of a Regency buck. Philippe, with his grace and poise, should have been wearing dazzling brocade, with ruffles falling over his strong, thin hands, a brilliant jewel stuck into a lace cravat. He was not like the usual man of the seventies, despite the sartorial excellence of his frock-coat and narrow trousers.

At first he greeted her in French, but Louis pleaded for English.

"We try to think of ourselves as English," he said, as he ushered them into the sitting-room. "We have lived here so long, it is our natural language now. Philippe is staying for a day or two, Regina, isn't that good news? Have you two ever met before?"

"No." It was Lavisse who answered, flatly and

uncompromisingly. "No, we haven't."

Regina felt a quick spurt of anger. The words were harmless enough, and true, but he had said them as if he were thankful that she had been no part of his world. As his eyes travelled over her, she felt he should have had a quizzing glass to complete the illusion that he was from another age.

"No." She confirmed Philippe's denial, wondering why she was so glad that she had decided to wear her new lilac dress, which hugged her figure like a second skin and then swept itself up behind into a becoming bustle trimmed with braid. "No, I've never met any of that side of the family, I'm afraid."

"Well, this is your chance to get to know at least one member." Louis's cheeks were almost pink with his excitement. "Ah, I think I hear Mrs Preece outside, and I must tell her to get Philippe's room ready. Excuse me, both of you."

The silence was leaden after Louis had gone. Regina didn't know what to say, and Lavisse shewed no sign of wishing to converse, the slumberous lids concealing whatever he was thinking. Finally, she said desperately:

"This is my first visit to England. Have you been here before? Have you met Aunt Marionette?"

"No and no."

The tone was short and discouraging, but she persevered.

"No, I hadn't seen her either until I arrived a few days ago. It's sad, isn't it, that she will never walk again?"

"No doubt she's grown used to it." He was not helping to ease the strain. Indeed, he appeared to be going out of his way to be difficult. "After all, the accident took place twenty years ago, or so my mother told me."

"Yes, that's true, but still ..."

"And how long do you propose to stay?"

She flushed, as if he were accusing her of pushing herself in where she wasn't wanted. Angry at herself for letting him put her at a disadvantage, she said briefly:

"Not long. And you?"

"Not long."

The conversation was killed off completely as they waited for

Louis to return, Regina forcing herself not to fiddle with the buttons on the bodice of her gown. She had already taken a dislike to Philippe, or so she assured herself, and it was equally clear that he had no time for her.

When Louis had come and collected Lavisse, Regina left the sitting-room too, at a loss to know what to do. Coffee would be served in the morning-room at eleven, but that was another half hour away. She considered the possibility of going to see Marionette, but something warned her not to do so without an invitation, and so she made her way upstairs to her own room.

Even at that time of the day the house seemed sombre. The snow had stopped, but the clouds were low, wrapping the world in their sad folds. She wished she could have gone down to the kitchen and watched Millie baking, listening to the servants chattering away as they did their work, but she couldn't do that. One duty call was acceptable: another, so soon, would be considered out of place.

She mounted the next flight, feeling as though she were not alone, trying not to look over her shoulder. In the end, she couldn't resist it, but there was nothing there, and she said a few words under her breath which would have shocked the innocent Louis had he heard them.

She went up the next flight, scolding herself roundly. She really must pull herself together. There wasn't anything wrong with the house. It was simply her imagination, fed by the things which the servants had whispered in their ignorance. How could there have been an eye on her aunt's bedside table? Marcelle had insisted on following Mrs Preece the night before, to assure herself that Reá had been lying, and, of course, there was nothing there. Just a tart word from the then awakened Marionette to Marcelle to go away and leave her in peace.

No, if there was anything wrong, it must be in her own mind. She was manufacturing the claustrophobic atmosphere herself, each tiny incident feeding the fable she was creating. Then she saw the door ahead of her close slowly and without a sound, and her heart missed a beat.

If she had seen the door shut, why hadn't she seen the person who had just gone through it? She almost ran up the five steps into the annexe. She hadn't seen anyone, for the simple reason that there hadn't been anyone there.

She sat on the window-seat, thankful that Tottie May had got a good fire going, for there•were chills running down her spine as she looked out at the blanket of snow covering the lawn below.

She couldn't see Louis's workshop, but she knew it was there, and all at once a thought sprang into her mind which made her put one hand over her mouth to stop any exclamation escaping.

After a second she was calm again, going to the mirror to smooth her hair, rubbing her cheeks to bring colour back into them. What a fool she was! How totally idiotic to entertain such an idea, even for a moment. She was getting as bad as Rea, thinking that one of the puppets, who borrowed people's souls, had slipped into the house and gone through a door on the floor beneath hers.

What would the others think of her if they had known what tricks her mind was playing? What would Philippe think?

What on earth did it matter what Philippe Lavisse thought? She raised her chin, all traces of nerves gone, as she made her way downstairs to join the others.

An hour later, and despite the cold, Regina went for a walk in the garden. Wrapped up well, even the January wind was better than the shadows inside. She snuggled her hands into her muff and braved the wild buffeting as she moved in the direction of Louis's workshop. She was determined to look at it again, accepting it for what it was. An ordinary wooden shed, with small windows and a padlock on the door.

The workshop was tucked into a corner of the garden, as if it were hiding. She hadn't realised on her first visit how secretive it looked, and her good resolutions were beginning to melt away when she saw the door open. Quickly she drew back behind the trunk of a large oak tree, watching cautiously as the door slammed shut again.

She saw Conrad Von Heltz running like the wind, catching a glimpse of his face as he rushed past her, her heart leaping again. Von Heltz had looked petrified, but why? She, Regina, might have felt a trifle nervous about Uncle Louis's life-like puppets seen by candle-light, but the German wouldn't, surely?

She knew Louis wasn't in the workshop, for she had seen him go down the garden path some while ago, muffled up and fastening the gate carefully behind him. In any event, dear Louis, with his vague-eyes and kindly charm, wouldn't have hurt a fly. So what could Conrad possibly have seen in there to produce so strong a reaction?

She had no intention of finding out, and began her own rather rapid return. She was almost at the house when a new thought struck her, and she paused. How had Conrad got into the shed; it was always kept locked. Had Eda Trott let him in? But there was no sign of the old seamstress, unless, of course, she was still in there, sewing the tiny garments for Louis's playthings.

"How brave of you to go walking on such a morning."

Regina almost jumped out of her skin as Philippe Lavisse moved from behind a clump of bushes and stood in her path. The heavy top coat did nothing to detract from his lithe grace, and he hadn't bothered to put on a hat, his hair stirring in the wind.

"Oh! You startled me." She was inane, and knew it, but she couldn't think of anything else to say, waiting until the shock had passed before she spoke again. "Did you see him?"

One thin brow rose slightly.

"Him?"

"Conrad. Did you see him go into the house? I thought you might have done. He looked so ..."

"I don't know anyone called Conrad." The lids were half-down again. "Oh, I suppose you mean Louis's German guest. No, I haven't met him yet."

"But he just went by." She felt frozen, wishing she could go indoors, but this was something she had to settle. "He was running from the workshop. He must have passed you."

"I can assure you that he didn't." The lips moved fractionally,

as if he were amused by her insistence. "You were saying he
looked …"

She coloured.

"It's nothing."

"Oh, but I think it is. You were most vehement about it a
moment ago. How did this Teutonic gentleman look?"

"I … thought he looked frightened." She didn't flinch from
his scepticism. "Very frightened indeed."

"Really?" He was more disbelieving than ever. "How
remarkable. Now, I wonder why anyone should find the good
Louis's workshop fearful."

"Have you seen it?"

"Only from outside. It seems harmless enough."

"I've been inside." She said it half to herself, almost forgetting
him for a moment. "I've seen the marionettes."

"And you didn't like them?"

"They're very cleverly made," she replied hastily. "Did Louis
tell you about his hobby?"

"At some length." Philippe was dry. "But cleverly made or
not, you didn't care for them."

It wasn't a question, and she didn't comment as he took her
arm lightly and led her back to the house.

"Understandable, perhaps, for you to find them somewhat
bizarre, but for Von Heltz to rush away from them as if the Devil
were after him is something rather different." The grey eyes met
hers, suddenly very penetrating and disconcerting. "You
probably imagined it, my dear Regina. The man was just cold,
and had had enough of the garden on such a day, as I have."

Regina didn't argue; it wasn't any use. Philippe would never
believe her, whatever she said, but she knew she had been right.
It wasn't the temperature which had driven Victor's friend
hurtling back through the shrubbery and over the frozen lawn. It
had been stark, unadulterated terror.

"Thank you," she said when they were back in the hall. "No
doubt I shall see you at luncheon."

"No doubt. We shall have to get to know one another, won't
we? After all, we are cousins of a sort, aren't we?"

Regina went upstairs and shed her coat. At first she flatly refused to entertain another unpleasant doubt which had crept into her mind. It was too utterly absurd. Just as silly as imagining the marionettes could leave the shed and get into the house. But the idea couldn't be shifted, however illogical it was.

Philippe spoke perfect French, and clearly he must have known a great deal about the family, for he had had a long talk with Louis, yet as she touched the lobes of her ears with a light perfume, the suspicion became a certainty.

The handsome man, whom she would have decked in powdered wig and knee-breeches, wasn't Philippe Lavisse. She was quite sure of it, although why she didn't know.

But if he wasn't the son of Marionette's cousin, René, who was he?

Regina awoke that night about two a.m. She had no idea what had roused her, but she got out of bed and pulled on a wrap. When she opened the door, she could hear the sound of voices, and other noises too, coming from the floor below. They were indistinct and muffled, for they were some way away from her annexe bedroom, but this time it wasn't imagination.

As she got to the first floor, she could smell burning; acrid in her nostrils and making her cough. The others were all there, crowding round the door of Von Heltz's room. Finally she got to the opening too, bewildered and unbelieving.

The bedroom was filled with smoke, making her eyes water as she watched Louis, Philippe and Victor beating out stubborn flames with damp cloths. Dummer was there too; brawny arms wielding an old coat against orange tongues. The three maids had produced pails of water, Rea crying with fear as she lugged a heavy bucket through the door and dumped it down beside Philippe.

Regina could see the remains of the curtains, charred and limp; the coverlet totally destroyed; the hangings round the tester shrivelled into narrow brown strips. Across what was left of the bed lay Conrad, eyes wide open, half his face burnt away.

She felt sick and giddy, but nobody noticed it. They were too busy fighting the last of the fire, making sure it was quite out before they straightened up.

"Uncle!"

Louis turned to her at last, his face grey.

"Oh my dear, you shouldn't be here. Don't come in, please. Go downstairs in the warm."

"I ... I ... can't. What happened? Herr Von Heltz ... is he ..."

"He's very dead," said Philippe baldly, oblivious to Victor's muffled cry of despair. "No doubt that was what you were going to ask. Marcelle, will you move please? I suggest you too take Louis's advice and leave us to clear up."

"But what happened?" Regina remained rooted to the spot. "How did the fire begin?"

"We're not sure, of course." Louis wiped his sooty brow with his handkerchief. But we did find part of a matchbox which somehow managed to escape the blaze. It was with Conrad's cigar-case, which was just recognizable. Also, Herr Von Heltz had asked Effie for a newspaper just before he went to his room. We think he was smoking in bed and dropped off into a deep sleep, letting the cigar fall on to the paper. It's the only explanation. Caleb, you'd better go for the police now."

"The police!"

"They like to know when people die in odd circumstances."

Lavisse remained immaculate, despite the work he had been doing, and Regina resented it. He was so detached, as if nothing ever got near to him. Again she felt the same strong presentiment that he was a stranger. Not of the family at all, but someone who had come to stay with it for some reason of his own.

He watched the expression of her face, smiling caustically.

"They would think it a trifle peculiar if we didn't inform them, wouldn't they?"

The police accepted Conrad's death as an accident. They shared Louis's theory of what had happened, and when they had asked their final questions and gone on their way, the remains of the dead German were removed to an empty room to await the undertaker's men. The family assembled round the sitting-room fire and drank hot tea served by Millie herself, since none of the other maids was fit to be seen.

"Like chimney sweeps," said Millie, giving Louis a bleak look as if it were his fault. "Can't 'ave them comin' in 'ere and makin' a mess."

"So careless," said Marcelle, when Mrs Butcher had bridled her way out of the room. "We might all have been burnt alive in our beds."

"As the luckless Conrad was." Philippe was sardonic. "Don't worry, Marcelle, you're safe enough now. Well, well, and here is your spouse. Denys, you've missed all the excitement."

Pritchard's face reflected the shock he was experiencing at finding everyone up, avoiding his wife's accusing eye as he began his lame excuses.

"Sorry I'm so late. Couldn't get a cab; bad weather, you know. What's happened?"

Marcelle told him in short sharp sentences, her lowering brow boding no good. Bad weather indeed! She could smell the cheap scent on him as he sat beside her. There was even a smear of lip salve on his collar. Did he think she was a fool? Couldn't get a cab! She turned from her husband and snapped at her daughter.

"What are you sitting there for, Jeanne? Go to bed at once. You'll be good for nothing in the morning, and heaven knows you're not exactly bright at the best of times." The sourness went as Jeanne fled, and Marcelle turned to Victor. "You go too, dear; you've had a tiring time. You must get your rest. It really is all very upsetting, and so inconvenient. It's not as if he had been one of the family. Such a nuisance, the funeral and all that. Perhaps we could get his body sent back to Germany."

"He was just like one of the family!" Victor was quivering with anger, standing up to his mother, his pale eyes daring her to deny it. "How can you say that he wasn't? You're a heartless old ..."

"That'll do, Victor!" Denys saw the chance of worming his way back into Marcelle's favour, and grabbed it quickly. They each knew the other was unfaithful, but he had just broken an unwritten law and got caught out. He had to make amends.

"Won't have you talking to your dear mother like that. As she says, the man wasn't one of us. Just a friend. Now, off to bed with you."

Victor flung himself out of the room, and Denys said uxoriously:

"Now, my love, you need some sleep too. You must be very upset."

Marcelle accepted the olive branch. After all, it was to their mutual advantage not to pry too closely into what one another was doing. As for Denys almost giving the game away by coming in stinking of his whore's perfume, well, she could exact a penalty for that next time he wanted some money.

"Yes, I am. Help me to bed, Denys, I'm quite exhausted."

Louis had gone to tell Marionette what had happened, and Regina and Philippe were left alone. She got up quickly, having no desire to engage in another verbal fencing match with him, when he said slowly:

"It seems you were right. Von Heltz was frightened, and with good reason."

She looked at him nervously.

"I don't know what you mean." The pulse in her throat was beating hard. "It was an accident. Louis said so; so did the police."

She said it rather too loudly, refusing to consider why the smell of the smoke, and the noise of the fire hadn't woken the German in time.

He studied her for a moment or two, dwelling thoughtfully on the remarkably coloured hair which was now hanging about her shoulders in thick, silky strands. Her dishabille made her look more vulnerable, the eyes like lapis-lazuli widened with the alarm in her. She was a beautiful creature, there was no question of that, but she had been on edge from the first moment he had seen her, although Von Heltz had only just been found dead. Why had she been so nervous before?

He wanted to touch her cheek and tell her not to worry, but she wouldn't have understood his gesture, and he wanted no complications. There was something far more important he had to do here than comfort Louis's niece.

"Good-night," he said finally, and opened the door for her. "Sleep well."

She passed him, turning her head to look at the grim line of his mouth.

"It really was an accident."

"If you say so, cousin dear," he replied calmly. "Good-night."

Regina met Rea on the stairs, still snivelling as she dragged one of the pails down the steps. She didn't really want to stop and talk to the kitchenmaid, for she was thinking of Philippe. She had seen his careful scrutiny, not too humble to recognise admiration when she saw it, but there had been something else as well. His look had been calculating, as if he were wondering whether she had had anything to do with the German's death. But that had been a dire mishap; it had to be.

"I told you," said Rea. "Didn't I say?"

"Say what?" Regina shook off the certain knowledge that Philippe had almost raised his hand to touch her. "What did you say?"

"I said someone was goin' to die, didn't I? Those crows came, remember?"

"But that couldn't have had anything to do with Herr Von Heltz's death." Regina was suddenly aware that apart from her candle, and the one in Rea's free hand, they were in familiar darkness again. Even death did not warrant the gasoliers staying alight a moment longer than was necessary. Considering Marionette was so rich, it was an odd foible; saving mere pennies on lighting the hall and stairways. "He'd been smoking in bed, you know."

"Maybe 'e 'ad, maybe 'e 'adn't, but 'e's dead, ain't 'e? I said someone was goin' to snuff it, and when I 'eard 'im quarrellin' with mistress, I knew it 'ud be 'im what went."

Regina held on to the banister rail, refusing to let Rea's words turn her legs completely to jelly.

"He quarrelled with my aunt?"

"Aye, they 'ad words right enough. I 'eard 'em with me own

ears, and I said then it 'ud be 'im. Soon as I 'eard what she said to 'im, I knew 'e'd be dead by mornin', and I was right, weren't I?"

She brushed past Regina, still crying as she thumped downstairs towards the kitchen. Regina stayed where she was for a whole minute, the candle wavering in the draught. Then she began the ascent, for soon Philippe would be making his own way to bed, and she didn't want him to see her. At the top of the first flight she looked back into the empty void. How could one feel such a strong attraction for a man, and fear him so at the same time? She shrugged impatiently as she walked along the corridor. Of course she wasn't attracted to him; how could she be? She hardly knew him. As to being afraid of him, that was equally nonsensical.

Up to the next floor, and the five stairs to safety. Inside her room she lit an oil lamp, wishing it wasn't throwing shapes on the wall, and that Rea's words would stop beating in her brain.

"I knew 'e'd be dead by mornin'."

Rea couldn't have known: she was just making capital of what had happened to draw attention to herself.

Regina turned to the bed to reach for her nightgown, stopping abruptly. At first, she didn't believe it. It was another illusion; it couldn't be true. It was like Rea's eye: just a trick of the light.

But when she blinked, it was still there. A doll, some two foot high, lying on her pillow, dressed in tweeds very much like those which Von Heltz had favoured, with real blond hair, and regular features moulded carefully in wax. The bright blue eyes seemed to be looking straight at her. They weren't just glass: glass couldn't mock as these eyes were mocking.

She put a hand over her mouth, convinced for a second that Rea was right. The dolls did assume the personalities of those whom they represented; taking their souls, as the kitchenmaid had said. Now this marionette had got Conrad's soul for good, and it was well pleased with itself.

With a cry of disgust, Regina forced herself to pick the thing up, carrying it at arm's length to the window, where she threw it out into the night. Only when she was trying to get warm under the blankets did the thought slither unbidden into her mind.

The puppet really had been on the bed. It hadn't been her imagination; it had actually been there, lying against her pillow. The question was, had someone put it there, or had it come in by itself?

Jeanne took off her dressing-gown and slid between the darned cotton sheets. The sight of Von Heltz's face was imprinted on her mind as if it had been etched there with acid. She had never seen a dead body before; never known what destructive fire could do to human flesh. The tea hadn't warmed her, and she could scarcely feel her feet, for they had grown numb.

She couldn't ask for a stone hot-water bottle, because she couldn't speak, and no one ever thought to ask if she needed one. To her mother, she was a nuisance; her father scarcely noticed her existence; the servants ignored her. She could feel tears under her closed lids. How she hated her mother. Fat, overblown, bombastic, without a shred of feeling in her body. Why couldn't it have been Marcelle who lay dead in the empty room downstairs?

She turned away from her wicked thoughts, only to find that she was envying Regina Curtis. So lovely that it was painful to look at her, and such exquisite clothes and jewels. Why did some women have so much, and others have so little?

Then she began to smile, Regina forgotten. Victor had looked shrunken when he had bent over Conrad's remains. Victor, who had bullied her for as long as she could remember. Victor, who even now, took secret opportunities to get her alone and inflict pain on her, knowing she couldn't call out for help. The smile became a grimace of satisfaction. Now Victor was hurting. His precious friend had gone. It seemed that God did sometimes punish the wicked, although not as often as He should have done.

The smile froze on her lips when she heard her door open, as she had done three times before. She had known it wasn't the end of it, and had lain awake for hours since the first occasion, listening for the turn of the handle.

She clenched her teeth as the soft footfall crossed to the bed. She was too paralysed to light the candle; besides, when the unknown visitor had first come, he had told her not to do so. He hadn't had to warn her not to cry out, because he obviously knew she couldn't do that, however great the panic grew. But he had breathed in a high-pitched whisper that she was never to try to see him if she wished to go on living.

The bedclothes were being drawn back, icy draught on her exposed legs as a hand lifted the shabby nightgown up to her thighs. She felt fingers stroking her gently, holding herself rigid like a plank of wood, stiff and unyielding as the hand explored higher still with an intimacy which made a mute scream rise in her throat.

She made the small moaning noise which was the nearest thing she ever got to speech, but it made no difference. She was being pulled up, the nightdress drawn over her head. She tried to push the thing away, but it was stronger than she, and furthermore it couldn't be human. It wasn't anyone who lived in the house; she was sure of that. It was something which Marionette sent to remind her of who was mistress. A creature from a place which Jeanne couldn't bear to think about.

She felt herself shuddering from head to foot. Whatever it was, it had adopted the guise of a human, at least in part, for it was a warm hairy chest pressed hard against her own, a strong male hand fondling her again and arousing a feeling in her which was far worse than fear.

She knew it was one of the puppets; it had to be. One to which Marionette had given life and movement, and made it as large as a man: one of those ghastly dolls which appropriated the souls of the unwary.

The mouth was over hers now, its weight smothering her as the preliminaries came to an end.

Even as her mind screamed a rejection, unconsciously her body began to respond. She tried to stop herself, knowing it was unnatural and terribly, terribly wrong, and that ultimately she would die for her sins, but she was too caught up with the creature's hunger to resist any longer.

When the climax came, it was abhorrent and wildly exciting at one and the same time. All sense of reality was gone, as the fever gripped her, her mind reeling when raw emotion and lust possessed her.

She was damp with perspiration when the thing rose from the bed and slunk to the door. She knew she ought to get up, and not lie there naked and glowing, with cold air caressing her, as the night visitor had done not long ago.

Then she was herself again, jumping out of bed in disgust and filling her bowl with water. Every inch of herself had to be cleansed, for she was defiled. The brief happiness and sensual contentment was gone, and she was racked with remorse and fear again.

Which of the puppets was it who had come to torment her? Which one had been sent to punish her?

Afterwards, staring into the darkness, she could feel the wetness on her cheeks. She couldn't even ask Marionette what she had done to displease her, so that she could make peace with her. But she must have done something dreadful to anger the bedridden woman.

Why else had the doll come?

Four

Regina was certain it was the song again. She had finally managed to get back into bed after the shock of Von Heltz's death, the puppet, and her worries about Philippe. It must be almost morning, and soon Rea would come with the tea-tray.

She couldn't be certain, for she knew she was upset, but as she crept to the door and opened it, she was sure enough. Deep and rich, like the notes of an organ; the same bitter-sweet melody.

Later, when Rea was putting the tray down outside, she called to her.

"Yes, Miss?"

Rea looked woebegone, eyes dull and heavy through lack of sleep.

"Did you hear anything about an hour ago?"

The maid's lids flickered nervously.

"What sort of thing?"

"Someone singing. Rea, you must have heard it."

"Not me, Miss." The tea was put down hastily, the girl almost running to the door. "I didn't 'ear nothin', but if you did, then it means she's angry again. Can't stop. Got to get the rest of the teas round. Tottie May's too upset, see, to manage the stairs."

Later, Regina answered Marionette's summons, and found Philippe already there, settled in an armchair by the fire. He looked as if he had slept a full eight hours, every hair in place, each garment fresh and spotless.

She took the stool by the bed.

"Good-morning, aunt. I hope you're well."

"Don't be a fool." Marionette was blunt. "How can I be well?"

"I didn't mean ... that is ... I ..."

"What do you know about this man's death?"

Regina met the shrewd black eyes, her heart sinking. It was almost as though Marionette knew that she had seen Von Heltz running from the shed, but that wasn't possible, unless, of course, Philippe had told her. She turned her head quickly to look at him, but he was gazing at the fire, relaxed and unaware of her doubts.

"Nothing. Nothing at all."

"Mm." Marionette's perpetual grin was in direct conflict with the tone of her voice. "Someone must know. Nothing like this has ever happened before."

"Hasn't it?"

Philippe was mildness itself, but Marionette was biting.

"What does that mean? Are you suggesting that my guests burn to death in their beds at regular intervals?"

"Hardly." Lavisse's laugh was soft and unamused. "The police would have asked a good many more questions if that had been so. No, I wasn't talking about Von Heltz. I was thinking of the servant who fell down the stairs, and the two companions who disappeared."

In the fire basket an applewood log spluttered. Marionette's face was livid.

"Who told you about them?"

He shrugged.

"I forget. One maid looks very much like another to me."

"I'll sack the lot of them, tittle-tattling imbeciles!"

"I wouldn't do that."

"Why not, pray?"

At last he looked at her, the smile satirical.

"Well, two of your servants have run off already, and another has pitched herself down the cellar stairs. If you get rid of those who are bold enough to stay, what will you do? Who will scrub and cook for you?"

"There are plenty of women I can get," she snapped, but

something flickered behind her eyes. "I'll manage, never fear."

"I wonder."

"You have no need to." The temper was gone. "I may let them stay, but I'll teach them not to gossip just the same."

Regina was apprehensive. A threat of punishment? How would Marionette teach her staff not to gossip? Stop their wages, or would she do something more drastic?"

"It was a dreadful accident," she said hurriedly, not wanting to dwell on alternatives Marionette might choose. "Poor man, his face was almost burnt away."

"Accident?" Marionette's laugh was harsh. "Is that what you think?"

Regina felt her mouth shrivel up.

"Well ... yes. What else could it be?"

"Ask him." Marionette tilted her head in Lavisse's direction. "He doesn't think it was, do you cousin?"

Lavisse didn't answer. He was looking at the fire again, taking no notice of them.

Marionette snorted.

"He won't put it into words, but you can take it from me he's not such a fool as you."

"But if it wasn't that ... what ..."

Marionette's concentration was on Regina now, and Regina had the same uncanny sense of being drawn towards the bed; as if Mme. Boussard had her by the wrists and was pulling her forwards.

Then the spell was broken, and Regina gave a small gasp. She was still on her stool, Marionette unmoving against her bank of pillows.

Regina wanted to ask Philippe if he had seen anything; felt anything. Glancing at him, she knew it would be no good. He wasn't paying attention to them, and even if he had been, he would deny any knowledge of what she was talking about.

"Forget it." Marionette suddenly waved a slender white hand, diamonds and rubies flashing in the light of the lamp by her side. It was almost dark outside; the clouds ready to pour forth another blizzard. "Put it out of your pretty head, child. Yes, call it an accident if you will. It's what those policemen said anyway."

The subject was changed, and there was some talk of Paris and the family, Philippe answering questions with an easy assurance which made Regina's mind cloud with doubt again. How could he know so much, if he were not who he said he was?

She forced her mind away from the subject, fixing her gaze on Marionette's rings. The stones were huge, and each time she saw Mme. Boussard, she wore a different selection. Regina could see beneath the folds of her shawl that Marionette even wore a diamond necklace: bluish-white, worth a fortune.

When Loveday Preece arrived with Marionette's tray, Regina and Philippe went down to the dining-room. There was a selection of cold meats, game pie, a hot dish of kidneys and mushrooms, with a choice of sweets and cheeses. Regina wasn't hungry, but she accepted a slice of ham and pretended to eat.

Her dread of Marionette was growing stronger. At first, she had been able to convince herself that it was mere fancy that the sick woman could harm others. Now it was different: a man had died. Lavisse didn't think the death was brought about by smoking in bed. Regina checked herself. No, that wasn't right. It was Marionette who had said Philippe didn't believe it.

Yet she must have thought him correct in his assessment, for she had been grinning, or had she? It was so difficult to tell when Marionette was really smiling, for the scar made the leer permanent. But if she had been amused, and Regina was inclined to think that she was, then had she contrived Conrad's end, as Rea claimed? Yet surely, if that had been so, wouldn't she have subscribed to the notion of an accident to cover whatever she had done?

The piece of ham Regina had in her mouth wouldn't go down her restricted throat. Could Marionette, lying helpless in bed, bring about the death of a man without stirring a finger, even daring to suggest afterwards that the cause was unnatural? And could she have sent the dead man's likeness to Regina's room as a warning?

But if it hadn't been Marionette who was responsible, who else could it have been? Regina flatly refused to dwell on what Rea

would have said. It was out of the question: they were nothing
but small pieces of wood, held together with screw-eyes, strings
attached to their arms and legs.

No, it couldn't have been one of them: it was quite impossible.

"Death attracts death, my gran always used to say." Noreen
Rutter was fussing round Denys late on the following evening,
pouring him a glass of beer. "That won't be the only one what
dies, luv, you see. Maybe it'll be 'er next. What's the chop like?"

"Very tender, ducks."

Noreen never objected to Denys's endearments, common or
not. Not a snob like Marcelle, but cheerful and compliant,
always ready to fit in with his mood.

"I got it special for you."

"Good of you. New curtains, I see."

Noreen looked pleased that he had noticed them.

"Yes, got them with that extra money you gave me. Nice bit
o' stuff, ain't it? Come from the market down the road. Makes
the room reel smart."

He nodded, letting his eye wander over the mantelpiece,
decently draped in a length of shiny crimson sateen complete
with bobbled fringe. His own photograph held pride of place,
next to two Staffordshire dogs, a simpering milkmaid, and three
vases of artificial flowers. He recognised that Noreen had no
taste, but then neither had he. This was how a real man's home
ought to be, not like that museum of a place in Chantry Close,
where one was afraid to tread on priceless Aubusson carpets, or
put a pipe down on polished mahogany tables.

"Yes, it's that right enough. A far cry from ..."

He broke off, but she knew what he meant.

"Never mind, pet." She sat herself on his knee, snuggling up
against him. "No need for you to think about that lot for an hour
or two."

"Mustn't be as late as I was last night." He sighed. "Marcelle
didn't like it when I came in with the others still up. She knew I
hadn't been to a concert, of course."

"Did she say somethin'?"

"No, there really wasn't time, what with that German being found dead and all, but she knew." He looked at Noreen soberly. He'd never actually admitted to her the tacit arrangement which he and Marcelle had between them; somehow it didn't seem proper. "I'd better get off about eleven."

Noreen pouted, but not seriously, for she knew how to manage Denys, and having the sulks was not one of the ways.

"So early? Oh well, that's not for ages yet. Maybe soon we won't 'ave to part like this, eh?"

"Maybe not, but sometimes I wonder if it won't go on for ever. Marcelle and the rest of 'em, I mean." He found himself lapsing into Noreen's cockney accent, not having to worry about the genteel vowels he'd had to master when he married Marcelle. "Gawd, what a thought."

"Don't think like that." She brushed his cheek with her lips. "You'll be shot of 'em soon enough. You're the clever one, you are."

He tried to smile, but his mouth was too stiff.

"But this is a bit different, isn't it? More to it than bein' clever, if you see what I mean."

"Aye, but if you're determined enough, you'll manage. You'll do it for me, won't you, Denys?"

Noreen had opened the collar of her blouse, and he could smell the mingled odour of her body and the flowery scent which she used. Both intoxicated him as he raised his hand to touch her breasts cradled in the stiff corset.

"Better get that thing off," he said huskily. "Can't see you proper like that."

She giggled.

"Want me, do you?"

"You know I do."

The blouse was opened a little further, pulled off the shoulders, tantalizing him.

"Then you'll 'ave to be brave for me, won't you?"

He licked lips, suddenly parched; hypnotised by the two white globes which looked like ripe fruit ready for the plucking. He didn't know what it was about Noreen's body which aroused the wild desire in him. He'd met enough dolly-mops like her before, God knows, but there was something different about Noreen when she took her clothes off. No other woman could make him sweat like she did, and none had given him such rich satisfaction.

"Soon. Get undressed."

"In a minute." She was torturing him now, deliberately leaning forward until she could see him perspiring. "Don't want to wait too long, you know. I'm not one to hang about for ever, Denys, not even for you."

He was almost in tears.

"Don't say that, Noreen! Don't never say that! You belong to me. You know I couldn't go on without you."

"Well, then." At last she relented, undoing the stays and pulling off petticoats with a practised hand. "You know what to do to keep me, don't you?"

She was purring, very sure of herself and her man.

"Yes, but ..."

Gently she took his hand, moving it until it was over one nipple, mouth to mouth as she drew him closer.

"You know, luv, don't you?"

"Yes." He was beaten, and they both knew it. "I know. Come upstairs."

They went up the narrow flight close together, bodies fusing into one. When he threw her across the bed and began to undress himself, she laughed, teeth like pearls against moist red lips.

"Promise, Denys?"

"I promise," he said thickly, throwing the last garment away from him. "Now come 'ere do, girl. You're drivin' me mad."

Regina shot up in bed about one o'clock. Although half-asleep, she still found time to consider how restless the house was after dark. It wasn't the first occasion she'd been woken suddenly; she was afraid it wouldn't be the last.

This time it was nothing mysterious, but Philippe Lavisse sitting on the short flight to the annexe, holding his ankle and swearing quietly but passionately to himself.

When Regina arrived on the scene, she found others there

before her. The noise had brought Tottie May, Mrs Butcher and
Marcelle to the second floor, and they were gazing at him in
stupified silence, until he said impatiently:

"For God's sake don't just stand there! Help me up."

"What happened?" Regina moved forward as Effie and Tottie
May got Lavisse to his feet. "I heard a noise."

"No doubt you did." He was still irritable. "I tripped over
something on these infernal stairs and twisted my ankle."

"I'm sorry." His tone made her own stiff. "Is it bad? I mean,
do you want us to call a doctor?"

"Hell, no!"

"Really, Philippe! Your language!"

He shot a scathing glance at Marcelle, her face greased and
bald-looking.

"I doubt if yours would be much better if you had just tripped
over something."

"That's the second time you've said that." Regina was holding
on to the newel post. "You didn't say you slipped: you said you
tripped. What did you mean?"

"For goodness sake, Regina, don't quibble." Marcelle was
crosser than ever. "What's the difference?"

"Quite a lot." Regina was looking at the stairs, lit up by the
servants' lamps. "There's nothing there to trip over now."

"Of course there isn't. What rubbish you do talk. Philippe
missed his footing, that's all." Marcelle turned to Effie. "Can you
bandage M. Lavisse's ankle?"

"Yes, Ma'am."

"Then do so at once. I'm going back to bed before I catch my
death of cold."

"What were you doing up?" Regina was still contemplating
the stairs, wondering about Philippe's words. "You haven't just
come in. You're in your dressing gown."

"So I am," he returned tartly, "and what I was doing out of
bed is scarcely your affair. Come, girl, if you think you can fix a
bandage without stopping the circulation."

When they were out of sight, Rea said at Regina's elbow:

"So, it 'appened."

Regina felt her hair stand on end.

"Good gracious, Rea, you scared me silly! I didn't know you were there. What do you want?"

"Nothin' Miss. Just heard noises, that's all. Come down after the others."

"Well now you'd better go back after the others." Regina was curt. The kitchenmaid's sudden appearance out of nowhere had made her nerve ends jump. "There's nothing you can do. Effie will see to M. Lavisse's ankle. He fell over some ... that is ... he slipped on the stairs."

"Yes, I guessed it were somethin' like that." Rea's face was bloodless. "I knew 'e was for it when I 'eard 'im arguing with 'er earlier on. I knew she'd pay 'im out and now she 'as. Never does to cross 'er, likes I told you. You always suffers in the end."

Caleb Dummer was sitting in the potting-shed the next morning, stuffing tobacco into a blackened clay pipe. Despite the weather, he wore only a shirt of green twill, sleeves rolled up, for he never felt the cold; dirty corduroys tied with string round the ankles above heavy, mud-caked boots.

The brown hair was untidier than ever, pensive as he struck a lucifer and applied it to the pipe. He should have been outside making a start on the rockery which his master had ordered, but another five minutes wouldn't hurt. There wasn't anyone about at that hour to check on his activities, and he wanted to enjoy the mug of tea and slab of gingerbread which Effie McGee had just brought to him. He'd rewarded her with a slap on her bottom, and a promise of worse to come, scornful as she'd flushed with delight, giggling as she pretended to flee from him.

Women! They were all alike, wanting only one thing. Funny how different they were in their ways, but the end object was always the same. He didn't really mind. Housemaid or lady, it was all the same to him. Effie gave him extra tea and cake; the other had given him money. He'd been quite shocked by her; never thought she had that kind of desperation in her. A right stuck up piece she was, until he'd torn off her clothes and taught her who was master.

He let his mind wander back to the rockery. Silly time to make one, but old Boussard had been insistent for some reason. Missus hadn't wanted it, so Loveday Preece had said. The housekeeper had stood there, four-square and glowering as she passed on the message, but he wasn't worried about the likes of her. They were old enemies, he and Loveday. Now and then they would have a battle of wills, but he always won when he stood up and towered over her. In the final analysis, Preece was scared of his strength and what he might do to her if she gave him too much lip.

He grinned to himself. He'd make the rockery whatever she had to say, and however unsuitable the season. The place chosen for it was right away from the house, in a small corner where few ever went. Certainly missus 'ud never clap eyes on it, that was for sure. The ugly smile widened.

Although a man with scant sympathy for his fellow beings, he was almost sorry for Louis Boussard: sorry and contemptuous. If he'd been Boussard, he wouldn't have let that crippled bitch order him about, and tell him what he could and couldn't do. True, she had the money, but that shouldn't have been important. When a woman married, everything she possessed became her husband's, or should have done. With the Boussards it was different. What missus had, missus held on to.

Trouble was, M. Louis had never stood up to her. Should have clouted her earlier on, before the accident. Brought her to heel with a bloody good hiding as he, Caleb, would have done. Then Louis wouldn't have had to creep about the house as he did now, filling in his time with those toys of his. What a way for a man to spend his days.

The tea was gulped down, the pipe knocked out. Well, if the poor bastard wanted a rockery, a rockery he should have. Let that old hell-cat upstairs say what she would.

Outside, Caleb paused to consider the boldness of his words, a slight shadow flitting across his brow. Was he really wise to defy her, even to please the master? Funny things were said about the missus; funny things happened round about her too, although he'd always pretended it was nonsense when the maids twittered nervously amongst themselves. Only last night that Frenchie had tumbled downstairs, and Rea swore he had said he'd fallen over something. Something which wasn't there when the others arrived.

He spat on the ground and cursed aloud. Getting as bad as those tarts in the kitchen, imagining goodness knows what. How could that shrivelled creature upstairs harm anyone from her bed? The whole idea was daft.

Dummer surveyed the stones and rocks thoughtfully. They were large and heavy, some piled up against the high brick wall, but that wasn't what was making him hesitate. He was strong enough to move these and another load like them besides. No, it was something else, but he couldn't put his finger on it. He looked round, seeing nothing but trees bending in the wind, the earth hard as iron. Take some digging to get a large enough hole to start, but Caleb was proud of his muscles. He'd manage right enough.

For a split second he thought he heard a voice. Just a faint whisper, but when he swung about again there was no one there, and his expletive shocked the empty air as he reached for his pick.

He must pull himself together. In another minute, he'd be imagining Rea's disembodied eye was watching him. He rubbed his hands together, took a firm grip of the tool, and raised it high above his head.

Damn the woman. He was going to make the rockery, and nothing she could do would stop him.

When Regina heard the sound of Victor's voice raised in anger, she hesitated outside the morning-room. She had no desire to intrude on a family squabble. Louis was obviously glad that she was there, but it was clear that the rest of them did not share his enthusiasm.

She frowned as Victor's roar continued. Why wasn't the other person answering him back? Were they so stunned by his venom that they had lost their voice? She knew the reason then, and as Victor stormed out, face like thunder, she slipped into the room and found Jeanne sitting at the table, hands over her face.

"Jeanne."

The girl started, jerking up so that Regina could see the tears and distress in the dark hazel eyes.

"Jeane dear, what is it?"

It was pointless to ask, of course, for Jeanne couldn't reply, but Regina went over and sat by her, reaching out to comfort her. Jeanne drew back at once, and Regina's hand fell to her side.

"I'm sorry," she said finally. "I didn't mean to interfere. It's just that I hate to see you so unhappy. Oh, how I wish you could talk to me and tell me what's wrong. Can't you write it down? Let me help you."

Jeanne shrank back yet again, cowering away as if it were Regina herself who was the cause of her agony.

"You want me to go." Regina said it flatly when the silence had lasted a full minute. "You don't want me here, is that it?"

Jeanne nodded quickly, turning her head away as Regina sighed.

"Very well, I'll go." She paused by the door. "If you change your mind and feel you need someone, come and see me. I know you can't talk, but you can write. Please come."

Jeanne waited until the door was shut. Then fresh tears rolled down her cheeks. It was tempting to accept Regina's offer, but she knew she couldn't. She blew her nose, trying to compose herself. She wouldn't dare to tell anyone about her secret. It wasn't like other people's secrets: it was dirty and sordid and terrifying. She stared down at her hands as if the shaking fingers didn't belong to her.

The first occurrence had been bad enough; now a new fear was assailing her. She'd wondered which of the puppets Marionette was using, but never before had she had a clue. Now she believed she knew. There had been something vaguely familiar about the whisper on the last occasion. She couldn't be absolutely certain, but she thought she was right.

Her teeth bit into her lower lip until it bled. If it were Victor's likeness which grew to life-size proportions once it got into the house, then what she was committing was incest. Her own brother! Well, not really her own brother, for he hated women.

Inexperienced and innocent as she was, Jeanne knew that. Victor had loved Conrad, and before that the boy, Jacob, who had been employed to help Caleb. When Victor and Jacob had been found together in the potting shed, Jacob had been sent away, and Victor had sulked for a week.

She sat up; erect enough to please even her mother. She knew she wouldn't be able to beat off the thing if it came again, but whatever happened she mustn't enjoy it any more. The ecstasy of that final moment must be resisted. Even if it were only a marionette, possessed of the Devil, it was still a miniature of her brother, and she must fight her weak and sinful nature.

If she didn't, she'd land in hell, and hell was where Louis Boussard kept his dolls.

Two days passed. No one, including Regina herself, had mentioned the question of her return to London. The matter seemed to have been forgotten, as if she'd come to stay for good. She told herself that her reluctance to leave had nothing to do with the presence of Philippe Lavisse, or whoever he was, but her self-delusions were becoming weaker.

She liked the house even less than when she had arrived, sensing something about it which was wrong, yet never being able to pin down the cause of it. There were footsteps very late at night. The first time she had got up to see who it was, she had found it was Denys Pritchard tip-toeing up to his room. His candle revealed complacent satisfaction on his face; like a well fed cat, replete with cream. Could music really do that to such a man? The next time it was Lavisse again, ankle well on the mend now. He was in a long blue robe, making his way downstairs.

She had peered through the open crack of her door. Where was he going? Her heart missed a beat. Was he going to a woman? She made a feeble attempt to laugh at herself. There weren't any women in the house likely to attract Philippe. The laugh curdled and died. Some men had odd appetites. Marcelle was not really old yet, and by candle-light and in the darkness ... who knew? And Jeanne; young and immature, with so much to learn of life and love. Many men liked virgins.

It wasn't only at night that nasty things occurred. Yesterday afternoon she'd heard the singing again, not bothering to ask if others had done so, for she knew they would deny it. It must be someone in Chantry Close, but why didn't the servants admit it? There was no harm in singing.

And only that morning Regina, going to her room to tidy herself for luncheon, had seen another door swinging to. She knew it was an unoccupied room, the one where Conrad's body had been laid before the men in black top hats had come to remove it.

She forced down her fears and knocked at the door. When there was no answer she had gone in, knowing that it would be empty. But it wasn't quite. Her legs had almost given way under her as she had clung to the post of the bed, trying to tear her eyes away from the doll lying on the coverlet. Red hair with a fringe; well-padded body, and tiny tiny beads round its rather thick neck. So, another puppet had got into the house.

She had got out of the room somehow, and had managed to sit through the meal without looking at Marcelle. She had wondered what Marcelle would say if she knew what was up there in that bedroom.

The next morning she woke with a splitting headache. Fresh air was the only cure, and she wrapped up warmly and let herself out of the side door. She'd heard furtive whispers about that particular door, but couldn't quite understand what Effie, Tottie May and the others were saying.

She walked briskly away from the house, right down to the end, where she looked boldly at Louis's workshop. Then she turned back. After a moment she noticed the small path leading off to the right. It was very slippery, but she kept her balance, finding herself after a moment or two in a small enclave: a garden within a garden. There seemed to be an awful lot of large stones and rocks, and some had obviously shifted. She moved a bit closer, not knowing why. Probably the force of the wind had dislodged them, for it was rough enough, whipping her skirts about her ankles as if it hated her and wanted to drive her off.

When she saw it, every drop of blood drained out of her face.

She forced herself to take another step forward, but there was no mistake. Between the fallen stones there was a human arm and hand sticking out, rigid and bleached white.

She screamed aloud, but the gale carried the sound away, and she had to run back to the house before she could raise the alarm and gasp out her story to Louis and the others.

They followed her quickly, grabbing at coats and scarves, hastening down the garden and finally pausing; a semi-circle of shocked faces as they stared at Regina's discovery.

"Oh my God!" Marcelle gave a moan. "Who is it? What's happened?"

Louis seemed too shaken to answer, and it was Philippe, leaning on his stick, who said tautly:

"It's Dummer. See, the hand is calloused, and there's just a bit of that green shirt of his shewing."

"Caleb!"

At last Louis spoke, his voice hardly audible. Regina saw his torment, and touched his arm, at precisely the same moment that another stab of fear went through her. Had Philippe been at Chantry Close long enough to see that much of Dummer, and to notice that he had worn a green shirt?

"This is my fault." Louis was stricken. "I killed him."

"You! Uncle, I don't understand."

"Don't be absurd!" Philippe was angry. "How could you have killed him? It's obvious what happened. He was working here, and these infernal stones weren't properly stacked. He was a strong man, but if they'd fallen without warning, he wouldn't have been able to get out of the way in time. Probably one struck his head. It would have been over instantly." He said something under his breath. "What a damned fool time to make a rockery anyway."

Rea burst into loud sobs, and Millie Butcher pushed her out of the way with a snap.

"Don't look, if it upsets you. Get back to the 'ouse and get the kettle on."

"It is my fault," said Louis again unaware of the gawping faces of Effie and Tottie May, which were as bloodless as Caleb's arm. "I told him to do it. Marionette hated rockeries. She said they were ugly and artificial and he wasn't to make one, but for once I defied her, and told Dummer to go on."

"That's right." Loveday was looking at the frozen fingers, but she wasn't even shocked. She didn't appear to be moved at all by the sight of the motionless limb. "Told Caleb meself not to. Said it was mistress's orders, but 'e only laughed, and said 'e was goin' to do it anyway."

"And you told your mistress what he'd said?"

Loveday gave Lavisse a look full of unpleasant knowledge.

"Yes, I told 'er."

"And what did she say?"

They waited for Loveday Preece to answer, every eye on her.

"She said she'd make 'im pay, of course. What did you expect?"

"I told you." Boussard was full of suffering. "That poor man. I should never have insisted. I should have known."

"But, uncle ..."

"For God's sake!"

Louis took no notice of Regina or Philippe.

"I told Dummer to do what Marionette had forbidden him to do. Oh yes, I'm responsible."

There were no comments for several seconds, the implication of what Boussard was saying lost on none of them. Slowly they turned to look in the direction of the house, hidden behind swaying poplar trees. It was just as if they were a group of Louis's puppets, their strings being tugged to make them move their heads in unison.

"Well," said Lavisse finally, "whatever the cause, we'd better call the police. They must be told what has happened."

Tottie May was despatched to the nearest station, whilst the others returned to get warm drinks.

Hugging herself by the hearth, Regina found that Louis's words would not leave her mind. They stuck there like burrs, refusing to be dislodged. She was trying desperately to be sensible, but it was so hard. There were too many things happening for common sense to win the day.

Louis believed that his wife had the power; the servants were sure of it; probably Marcelle was beginning to wonder; Jeanne certainly thought so, or why else was she so afraid? Everyone was whispering it, either to each other, or inside themselves, and now she, Regina, was beginning to believe it too.

Marionette Boussard was most definitely not as others were. Marionette must be a witch.

Five

When the singing started the next night, Regina wanted to scream. It was so weird and so inexplicable. She knew that it was not a noise in her own head, for the servants had heard it too, but they all swore that it was no one in the house who was responsible.

They did not seem to understand how macabre their assurance was. If it wasn't one of the women of the house, yet the voice was within No: 7, Chantry Close, then it must come from another world, and only when Mme. Boussard was angry.

Regina got out of bed, furious with herself. Of course, it wasn't from another world; it was one of the family or the servants, and this time she was determined to find out who it was, and why they were doing such a thing.

By the time she had reached the lower landing, it had stopped, but leaning over the banister rail she could see the back of a tall, dark man in the hall. He was turning right, along the passage which led to the side door. It must be Philippe; it couldn't be anyone else. She was still wondering where he was going, when she saw Marcelle appear, moving in the same direction.

Marcelle's candle threw its flame on to her face, and creeping down the stairs as silently as a ghost, Regina could see the heavy cosmetics on the plump face and the low-cut peignoir of velvet with lace cuffs.

Her legs gave way, and she sank down on one of the treads. Philippe and Marcelle! Was it possible? She'd wondered before whether Lavisse could have found Denys's wife attractive, and had tried to dismiss the idea as a nonsense. But the expression on

Marcelle's face was not hard to interpret. She was going to a lover, bedaubed and besotted, exuding, even from a distance in poor light, an aura of lust. How could Philippe! Marcelle was old and fat and … Regina pulled herself up. Not so old, and some men like a Junoesque figure, particularly one with skin the colour of milk.

But if Philippe and Marcelle had arranged to meet, why were they going out of the house? Goodness knows there were enough spare rooms in which to conduct their illicit *affaire*.

Wearily, Regina rose to her feet. Perhaps some small spark of decency remained in one or other of them, and they couldn't bring themselves to make love under Marionette's roof. There were plenty of sheds and outhouses, and Regina wished them joy of them, hoping the pair would freeze to death.

It was then, pulling the clothes over her head and shutting her eyes, that she had to admit to herself something she had been trying hard to avoid. Whether Lavisse was who he said he was or not, it didn't matter. She wanted him as urgently and desperately as Marcelle did, and if she had had to lie in his arms in an icy barn she wouldn't have cared a jot. Damn Philippe, and damn Marcelle too.

The well-bred, self-controlled, sophisticated Miss Curtis turned her face into her pillow and cried herself to sleep.

She knew she was a fool to start questioning Philippe on the following morning, for the risk of giving away her own thoughts was too great, but the small demon inside her, goaded by jealousy, would not let her rest.

"Did you notice anything during the night?" she asked innocently.

They were the last at the breakfast table, Philippe drinking coffee, Regina deliberately prolonging her meal by nibbling toast and marmalade which she didn't want.

"I thought I heard that voice again."

He was quite disinterested.

"Did you now? How very disturbing for you."

She bit back her retort, striving to keep calm.

"Yes, it was rather. I thought you must have noticed it too, since you were up."

"Up?"

"Yes." She had burnt her boats now, and she didn't care. "I came down to find out who it was, and I saw you. You were walking towards the side door. What were you doing?"

He looked at her silently until her cheeks were scarlet with embarrassment. She had gone too far, and she knew it. Finally he said:

"You're wrong. I wasn't near the side door last night. In fact, from eleven onwards I was in my bed, as you should have been in yours."

"I ... I ... must have been mistaken, but I was so sure." She wouldn't give him the satisfaction of seeing her tears of mortification. "You and Marcelle ... I was so certain."

"Marcelle?" His tone was sharper now. "You think you saw her too?"

"I'm sure I did. She was going to the side door as well."

The thin hard lips moved ironically.

"Are you match-making, my dear Regina, or accusing Marcelle of infidelity?"

"No, no, of course not." She denied it quickly, having no other choice. "I must have been dreaming."

"Most probably." He rose from the table. "If that is the turn your dreams are taking, it's high time you were married, but be kind enough to leave me out of your fantasies in future."

She couldn't help the tears after he had gone. She wished he had hit her; it would have hurt much less. Then she blinked the sorrow away as Tottie May came in to clear, leaving the breakfast-room hastily in case those yellowish eyes saw the grief.

But had she been dreaming, or was Philippe lying? She wished she could have accepted the former theory, but she couldn't. It was no use pretending to oneself, whoever else one tried to fool. It must have been Philippe Lavisse who had been downstairs last night; there was no other tall, dark man in the house.

And Marcelle had been there too, large as life, her perfume hanging in the air. No, there was no mistake: Lavisse had been lying.

Later that day, just before the hour of four, Regina went up to the attics. She couldn't settle to read a book, and no one else seemed to be about, so she decided to continue her unfinished exploration of the house.

On one side of the top floor the servants had their quarters, and these she avoided, turning to the other wing where she found four empty rooms, some filled with trunks and old furniture, and one with nothing more than dust and cobwebs.

It was in this one that she paused, going over to the window seat to peer down into the garden. It looked a long way off, but from there she could see the roof of Louis's shed, and the quiver began again.

To take her mind off the workshop, she ran her hand along the cretonne seat, grimacing at the dust. No one bothered to clean up here, since the rooms weren't used, and in the wintry light the place was sad and forlorn.

Almost without thinking, she lifted the lid of the seat, her mouth opening slowly as she stared down into the space below. It was a few minutes before she could muster the necessary courage to reach down and pull out the frock, holding it away from her as if it could do her physical harm.

It was not very old, despite its crumpled condition, but it wasn't that which was taking the colour out of her cheeks and making her shake in earnest. Finally, she moved nearer to the window, so that she could look at the front of the gown more closely.

She assured herself stoutly that the great blotches were caused by something like spilled gravey, or blacking from the stove, but she knew it wasn't so. She wanted to thrust the garment back from whence it had come, but she had to be sure, and so she moistened her finger, rubbing it hard on the marks, staring at the pink colour left on her skin.

She slammed the cover of the window seat down, the dress

hidden once more. It must belong to one of the servants; one who had cut her hand, perhaps, and decided that the frock wasn't worth cleaning. But so many stains, and such large ones.

When she got to the sitting-room, she paused. Did Marionette know what was hidden in the window-seat? With a sinking heart, Regina opened the door. Of course she knew: Marionette was probably responsible for it being there.

Now the attics were as frightening as Louis's workshop, but they still drew Regina to them. Late that night she sat on the side of her bed, knowing that something was willing her to go up there again; fighting the pull as hard as she could.

She hoped that no one had noticed her silence at dinner time. They hadn't appeared to do so; Philippe conversing now and then with Louis; Marcelle complaining that the chicken was overcooked; Jeanne staring down at her hands as usual; Victor pale and grieved as he pushed his food about his plate. Denys never did pay any attention to her at meal times; he was too busy eating.

At last she could resist the urge no longer. She wasn't sure whether it was she herself who felt impelled to go back to where she had found the dress, or whether it was Marionette who was forcing her, with the same power which she had appeared to use twice before.

On the top landing she could hear Effie's snores. The servants worked hard, good though their situations might be. Up at five-thirty every morning, never sitting down for a moment except when they gathered round the white wood table to eat their meals, or have a hot drink. They slept like the dead, letting nothing interfere with the few hours of precious rest they were allowed.

Slowly she went towards the empty rooms, back into the one with the window seat. It was cold, like a grave, the draught from the latticed window making the candle flutter until she thought it would go out. She had to look again; just once more. She was tense as she raised the lid and bent down. Then she gave a cry, letting it fall with a dull thud.

The dress was gone. It was no longer tnere: just an empty, dusty space. She swung round, sure that the noise she had made would bring at least one of the staff running in to see what was going on, but it seemed that their exhaustion was too great to be disturbed by so small a thing.

She was standing by the window, not knowing what to do, when the footsteps began. There was no carpet at this level, just worn linoleum, and the sound of the tread was quite clear in the stillness? Effie? Loveday Preece? Tottie May?

Somehow, Regina knew it wasn't them, or Millie or Rea either. She snuffed the candle out with her thumb and forefinger, not daring to stir as the intruder grew nearer. She had left the door open, but in the pitch darkness it was impossible to see whether anyone had come through it or not. Then, all at once, she knew someone had, for the feeling of no longer being alone was too strong to ignore.

She opened her mouth to ask who it was. Philippe? Uncle Louis? Victor? Denys? No, it couldn't be any of them, for they would have spoken. Her lips closed tightly. Whoever or whatever was in the room with her was not friendly. She was as sure of that as she had ever been of anything in her life. Drawing back against the wall, she heard a board creak under her foot, realising that the other would have heard it too, and would know where she stood. Yet she couldn't move. Nothing would make her legs move, nor force her feet to obey the insistence of her mind which was telling her to run.

It was nearer now, whatever it was. Human, or at least in human form, for she could hear it breathing; feel it close to her.

She went rigid as a hand slipped itself into her peignoir and began to fondle her. Her terror was so great that she couldn't strike the intruder away, nor twist aside from the degrading assault on her body. She could only remain as she was: not moving, not speaking as the fingers caressed her with a familiarity which made her brain reel with shock.

It was several minutes later that she realised it had gone, and she was alone again. She could still feel the touch of its hand on her, and wanted to be sick, but now she found enough strength to get to the door and grope her way downstairs, step by step, until she was in the safety of her own room.

The gasoliers were on, and the fire still glowing. She piled more coal on to the embers, and then rinsed her hands and face. The water was like ice, but she didn't even notice it, and then, all at once, she found herself tearing off her wrap and nightgown, washing every part of her body until she was sure no trace of the unknown person's hand was left.

She went over to the long mirror and considered herself with care. She looked just the same, as if nothing had happened, save that her eyes were huge, with smudges under them; cheeks the colour of chalk.

Who had been up there with her? She went on staring at herself whilst she thought about it, but no answer came. She wished she could have gone down to Uncle Louis's room and sobbed out her misery on his shoulder, but it wouldn't be fair to him. He had so much to worry him, and he was obviously far from well. In any event, even to Louis, how could she talk of what had just happened? His embarrassment would have been even more overwhelming than her own.

At last she took out a clean nightgown and slipped it over her head, getting into bed and leaving the lights on.

She wondered what Rea would have made of it, if the kitchenmaid knew what had gone on up there in the empty attic. The last trace of pinkness faded from Regina's lips as the response came back like a winged arrow. Rea would have said it was a marionette; one which had escaped from the shed.

Regina pressed finger-tips to her mouth to stop any sound escaping. Two dolls had got into the house already. Why not a third?

"But surely you could 'ave done somethin' about it by now?"

Noreen Rutter was plumping up gaudy coloured cushions on her sofa, casting a black look at Denys as he sank back into his favourite chair. She was growing increasingly impatient, for Denys shewed no signs of getting on with the job.

"Well no, lovey, I really haven't been able to do much, what

with the German dying like that, and then the gardener bein'
found under that pile of stones."

"Don't see what that's got to do with what we talked about."
She was unmoved by his excuses, lips condemning. "Police said
they were accidents, didn't they? So why should what happened
stop our plans? Seems to me you're not really tryin', and you
know what I've told you."

Then he saw her irritation, and his complacency vanished
quickly. He hadn't realised until that moment that her pencilled
brows were twitched together, and that she was looking at him
with something approaching dislike. He sweated a bit, for
whatever happened, he couldn't lose Noreen.

"You're right; maybe I've been a bit on the cautious side." He
placated her, taking her hand between his. "Didn't want to take
any risks for your sake."

"Nor your own, I'll be bound."

She was still not entirely appeased, but the frown was lifting.

"Promise you'll try soon."

"I promise. It won't be easy, but ..."

"It's her or us."

"I know."

"Then what'll it be?"

"Us, of course. Here, give us a kiss."

"Don't know that you deserve it."

She was fast relenting. She was really quite fond of Denys,
even if he was weak, impressed by the way he dressed and some
of the things he knew. Almost like a gent, in fact. Anyway, there
wasn't anyone to take his place, and Noreen was not one to
throw dirty water away until there was clean to be had. Besides,
if Denys could pull it off ... She sat on his knee, her mouth
against his.

"There you are; that better? Where will we go when it's ...
well ... when it's done? Paris? I've always wanted to see Paris."

"No!" he was almost hysterical. "No, not there. Anywhere
but Paris."

She was startled for a second at his outburst; then she
understood.

"Oh, 'cos she's French, you mean? All right, I don't mind, as long as it's away from here."

"I'll miss it, in a kind of way."

She jeered at him.

"Miss Lambeth? You're cuckoo. What's there to miss about Lambeth?"

"It's where I first met you."

She warmed to him, leaning against him, laughing softly.

"Why, you're romantic, d'you know that, Denys Pritchard? Well, I do declare. Still, we're not stayin' 'ere, that's for sure."

"No, no, it wouldn't be safe, after ... that is ... not after ..."

"No, it wouldn't. Like another beer?"

"Don't mind if I do." He watched her body move in fluid grace as she got up to fill his glass, mentally undressing her. Soon, if she were in a really good mood, she'd let him do it in reality. It was a special treat, offered to him only now and then. Mostly she took her own clothes off when they were ready for lovemaking, but every so often he was privileged to undo the buttons, drawing the gown from her shoulders, clumsy as he fumbled with the corset whilst she laughed at him. Then the more intimate garments, warm in his hand as he let them fall to the ground. He wondered if she'd let him do it to-night if he renewed his promise. "You won't ever leave me, Nor, will you?"

"Don't suppose so." She grinned over her shoulder. "Got sort of used to you."

"And you do love me?" He was still anxious, needing reassurance. "You do, don't you?"

"Aye, an' I'll love you more when you've ..."

"Yes, yes, I've promised. I've said I'll do it."

She came back to him, smiling down at him, but behind the smile there was a measure of impatience. She'd still have to go on stiffening his backbone, or the job would never get done. Nagging him wouldn't help, but something else might.

Her tongue moistened her lips as she put the glass down.

"Want that, do you, pet, or would you rather ..."

He got up quickly, still uncertain that she meant it.

"You mean you'll let me ..."

"Why not? You've been a good boy, haven't you? Special reward like, eh?"

He'd got the frock off, his hand shaking as he began to untie the strings of the corset, when she said casually:

"When do you think you'll do it, luv?"

On the following Thursday, Louis Boussard put on the promised puppet show. Regina didn't want to go, for by now she was really afraid of the dolls, irrational though she knew her fears to be. But she couldn't hurt Uncle Louis by refusing, and she certainly didn't want the supercilious Philippe to guess that she was scared of mere puppets.

The workshop was *en fête* that night. Covers had been placed over the work benches, concealing all the tools of the trade. On this special occasion it was simply a theatre, with the family taking the front benches, the servants shuffling into the back rows.

"It's very cold in here." Marcelle was complaining as she pulled a fur wrap about her shoulders. "Really, I don't know why I came. It's all so childish."

"Oh, I don't know, m'dear. Makes a change, and we wouldn't want to offend the old man, would we?" Denys took his own seat, his mind on Noreen. That last visit had been bliss, but the bliss had to be paid for, and he was gnawing his lip. He'd told Nor it wouldn't be easy, and it wouldn't, but he'd have to do it, somehow. "It'll soon warm up when the braziers get going."

"It's absurd." Marcelle was still irritated, totally blind to the expression on her husband's face as he looked at her. "Why can't he find something else to do? Jeanne! Do sit up! If I've told you once, I've told you a thousand times."

Jeanne didn't answer, sitting up straighter, but keeping her head bent so that the others wouldn't see her desperation. If only her mother would leave her alone. The nagging went on day after day, week after week, month after month. And it wasn't only the grating criticisms. Now and then, when her mother was especially angry, she would go to Jeanne's room, temper mingling with an odd sort of excitement. Lying across her bed, Jeanne accepted the stinging cuts of the cane in silence; there was nothing else she could do. But the shame of having her skirts pulled up to her waist as if she were a child, feeling the spiteful blows on her bare skin made her hatred of her mother swell until it almost choked her. If only Marcelle realised how violent her passion was, perhaps she would leave her alone but she, Jeanne, couldn't tell her.

When Regina saw the woman come from behind the stage and take her seat amongst the servants, she was puzzled. The newcomer was about thirty, with hair the colour of ripe corn, and large brown eyes. Her cape was thin and plain, the dress beneath shabby, but her body was as rich and inviting as the earth itself.

Regina turned to whisper to Effie McGee.

"Who is that? The woman sitting on the end of the bench behind you?"

"That's Mrs Trott."

Regina felt a violent sense of shock. That was Eda Trott, the seamstress who dressed Louis's children for him, and whose husband beat her when he was drunk? She ventured to turn her head again, somehow angered by the serenity of Eda's beauty. Thinking back, Louis had never said the woman was old: she, Regina, had just assumed it.

There was no time to think about the sewing-woman any more, for the curtains were parting, the audience settling down in the dimness of colza lamps and a few candles to watch the performance.

In spite of her repugnance and growing panic about the marionettes, Regina could not help but admire the skill with which Louis made them move. He even gave them voices; some high-pitched, some growling, some sweet and low. There were ballerinas in billowing tutus, cocking their heads as they glided over the stage; a skeleton which miraculously came apart, and, even more unbelievably, got itself together again in the space of a minute; a sailor doing a horn-pipe, and the clown which she had seen before.

After that, there was a pantomime. It was Cinderella, with each character dressed exactly according to the fairy tale; even a gilded coach moving smoothly on tiny wheels.

When there was a brief interval, Regina glanced at Philippe, but he was watching Eda Trott. She hated him for it, waiting impatiently for the curtains to part again so that she did not have to wonder why Philippe was so interested in a servant.

The final scene made Marcelle gasp in outrage. It was a perfect replica of the Boussard's dining-room, with a miniature Effie jerking in, balancing a tray; a forlorn Jeanne sagging in her chair.

"Don't slump like that, Jeanne."

The marionette which looked exactly like Marcelle raised a censorious hand. So, somehow the puppet had found its way back to the shed. Regina felt a grue.

"Sit up, girl, or you'll get round-shouldered."

There was the sound of smothered laughter from the servants until Marcelle turned round and hissed at them to be silent. Then it was Victor's turn; the mimicry so perfect that Regina had to pinch herself to make sure it was not Marcelle's son who was speaking. She prayed it would stop soon. The dolls weren't dolls at all. They were too real. Even the voices seemed to be coming out of their mouths, no matter which part of the stage they were on.

Finally it was over, and Marcelle rose majestically and swept to the door.

"Disgraceful," she announced in a loud voice. "I can't think what Louis was doing, making us look such fools in front of the staff. Come, Jeanne, don't dawdle; Victor, come along. We're going back to the house this very minute."

Regina lingered a moment longer to watch Philippe talking to Mrs Trott. Eda was smiling up at him, nodding. When Regina could bear it no longer, she hurried after Marcelle and the others, taking her place round the fire, waiting for Effie to bring in refreshments.

"It was in very bad taste." Marcelle was still upset, searching in her beaded purse for smelling salts. "I don't know when I've felt more mortified."

"I'm sure uncle didn't mean to upset you."

Regina tried to defend Louis, and got shouted down for her pains.

"Easy enough for you to say, seeing he didn't make a laughing-stock of you."

Regina subsided. It was true. Although Louis had said he would make a model of her, he obviously hadn't done so yet, nor of Lavisse either, and she thanked heaven for it.

Boussard and Lavisse came in together, Louis looking rather sheepish as he listened to Marcelle's tirade.

"I meant no harm," he said apologetically. "I wouldn't distress you for all the world. It was just a bit of harmless fun."

"It was not in the least funny," she retorted. "I cannot imagine what you were thinking about."

When Regina met Rea in the hall, she said doubtfully:

"It was cleverly done, wasn't it? The puppets, I mean."

"Them devilish things?" The girl looked more stricken than ever. "Not natural if you asks me."

"I thought them very realistic."

"Don't mean it that way. Unnatural for 'er to use 'em to punish people like she does, nor that they ..."

Her voice trailed away, and then she turned and ran.

Just as Regina was nearing the first floor, she encountered Loveday Preece.

"Real life-like were they, Miss?"

Loveday hadn't been present, but by the sneering expression on her face, Regina guessed that she had heard all about it.

"Very." She refused to let the woman's insolent tone get under her skin. "Goodnight, Mrs Preece."

"She's angry about it. Right put out."

Regina turned on the stairs.

"She?"

"Madame, of course. Don't like master to put on them shows."

"That is a matter betweeen them. It is none of our business."

"Ain't it? Well, we'll 'ave to see, won't we?"

She waddled off in the direction of Marionette's room, and Regina fled to the annexe. She would have some difficulty in getting to sleep that night. It wasn't only that she couldn't get it out of her mind that the dolls were growing more daring; there was also the recollection of Philippe and Eda Trott to keep her awake.

She blew her candle out quickly, and, for the second time, cried herself to sleep because of the hateful M. Lavisse.

Much later that night, Eda Trott stood by the truckle bed waiting. It was almost dark, for he said he didn't like much light, and she didn't question his preferences. She was a patient woman, not given to fussing about the passing of time, but when she heard footsteps, she smiled to herself, touching the thick veil of gold, now loose about her shoulders.

When she saw the dim outline of the man, her smile grew deeper and more satisfied.

"I'm glad you came back. I wasn't sure whether you would."

"I promised, didn't I?"

It was a whisper, deep and husky.

"Yes, but I still wasn't certain."

The laugh was barely audible as he patted her cheek.

"Don't you think you're worth coming back for?"

She was demure, eyes downcast.

"It's not for me to say."

"Then I'll say it for you. You're well worth it. How sensible to have a bed here."

"Yes, isn't it? Do you want me to undress?"

"Later. Let's talk for a while."

She complied at once, nothing ruffling her composure as she sat down.

"Where's your husband to-night?"

"In the King's Arms, I expect, dead drunk."

"Rather late for that."

"Then he's in a gutter somewhere." She said it indifferently, as if she was announcing that he had gone for a walk. "Perhaps someone will find him in the morning."

"You won't go home yet, will you?"

"No, not to-morrow. I've more work to do."

"Then you'll be safe."

"Yes, I'm always safe here."

The man took her face between his hands, studying it by the last flicker of the candle which remained alight.

"So lovely," he breathed softly. "Exquisite."

She didn't blush, nor shew any other form of embarrassment, remaining perfectly still, awaiting his further orders.

"Now, I think." The voice was quieter than ever. "Yes, now we'll make love, if you are ready."

Regina woke up with a sore throat. She lit her candle and glanced at the clock in dismay. Only three a.m., and ages before the arrival of morning tea. Yet she had to have a hot drink; something to soothe the rawness, and to get her off to sleep again.

In the kitchen, she warmed milk in one of Millie's pans, getting out a mug and finding the sugar bowl. It was whilst she was opening a drawer in search of a spoon that she saw the light coming up the garden from the direction of the shed. Quickly she put out her candle and drew the pan off the range. Then she crept back to the window to watch.

The man passed the window, his lantern illuminating black curling hair for a brief second as he went on his way to the side door.

Philippe! Regina struck another match, and went back to the milk, throat almost closed with pain. No need to guess why he'd been at the workshop so late. Uncle Louis had said that Eda Trott often slept there to get away from her husband.

By then, Regina had dismissed the idea that Philippe was interested in Marcelle. It was a thought too silly to entertain for long, and it was only because of the strong unwelcome feelings he aroused in her that she had ever considered it at all. But Eda Trott was a very different story. She was truly sensuous, and any man would want to make love to her.

There were tears in Regina's eyes as she sipped her drink, finding it difficult to swallow, troubled as she began to wonder again about Lavisse.

In the morning, she asked Louis a few tentative questions.

"René? Marionette's cousin? Oh yes, she worshipped him. He was very much like Jules Marigny, you know. René was a puppeteer too. She had left him a lot of money in her Will."

"But ... but isn't René dead?"

"Alas, yes." He turned short-sighted eyes on her, shrugging regretfully. "Marionette was heart-broken when she heard the news, and she altered her Will at once, so he shouldn't be forgotten."

"I don't understand."

"Well, she left it to his son instead. One day, Philippe will be a very rich man. Marcelle hopes that she will get the lion's share, but she won't. My wife has arranged for me to be well provided for; the rest is for Philippe."

Regina went into the morning-room, glad to find that no one was there. She needed time to be alone and to think. She was still convinced that the man who called himself Lavisse was an imposter, although there wasn't a shred of evidence to prove it. He knew so much about the family, that she must be wrong, yet still her instinct told her she wasn't. What she hadn't been able to understand was the man's motive for coming to Chantry Close, pretending to be a member of the family, and now Louis had furnished her with the answer.

What had happened to the real Philippe she had no idea, but now the false Lavisse was here, and one day he'd be a wealthy man. She put her hands round her throat, wishing that it would stop hurting so. Before he could inherit, Marionette would have to die.

Was that why he had come? To kill Marionette Boussard?

Six

It was nearly midnight before the servants got to bed on the night of the puppet show, for it had delayed the usual routine. Millie Butcher had been snappy with all of them as she hustled them about, giving directions as to the preparation of drinks, the final clearing of the kitchen, and getting coal up ready for a flying start in the morning.

Rea shared a small room with Tottie May. Tottie May's seniority earned her the rather shaky bed by the window; Rea had a truckle bed on the other side of a rickety table which held their alarm clock and candlesticks. They managed with one chair between them, a row of pegs near the door, and a wash-stand, complete with a plain white jug and bowl.

The lino was old and icy as Rea hopped into bed, but she hardly noticed it; she was too exhausted. She had to be up at five every day, because hers was the unenviable task of coping with the range. It was her enemy; needing its cinders sifted every blessed morning, its stubby body coated with Wellington blacklead which cost twopence a block. She was drifting off, thinking of what else she had to do when she got up in a few hours time. Emery paper for the steel fender ... white stone for the hearth ... scrubbing the kitchen and scullery floors ... acres of hard, cold flags ... the back stairs ... the larder ... hot water ... strong soap ...

Rea was off, breathing deeply in rhythm with her room-mate.

When she woke, it was very suddenly and very shockingly, and for a second or two she remained motionless, not believing what was happening. She wasn't in the narrow bed with its thin blankets, and there was no sound of Tottie May's customary snores.

Instead, she was in the garden, near master's workshop, her teeth chattering as the wind lashed at her for daring to be out at such an hour. The discovery of finding herself there made her legs weak, and for one dreadful moment she thought she was going to faint. Then she held on to a nearby bush, and forced herself to remain upright.

How had she got there? The last that she could remember was rubbing her frozen toes together to try to get them warm, thinking about the mountain of chores which awaited her, wondering if she would get through them before Mrs Butcher called them in for a breakfast of fried beef sausages, slices of cold meat, and thick hunks of bread.

She turned her head, in case there was someone else about who had carried her into the garden, but there wasn't. She had walked there by herself, in her sleep. She whimpered, remembering that her ma had told her how her gran used to sleep-walk, and how the half-mad old woman had finally got herself out on to a roof, plummeting down into the backyard where she had lain like a heap of rags.

Rea clenched her teeth to stop the noise they were making. She must get back to the house before she died of cold. It was the first time she'd done this, or was it? Had she walked at night before, and not known it? She was preparing to run when she saw a glimmer inside the shed. It was very faint, but it was there.

Rea's bare feet could hardly carry her to the workshop, but somehow she managed it. Who could possibly be there, and awake, at this hour? It must be after two o'clock; perhaps even later.

There was only one window low enough for Rea to peer through, but it gave a good view of the area where Mrs Trott worked and slept some nights to get away from her husband. Proper brute he must be. When Rea had heard about what he did to his wife, she swore to herself that she'd never marry. Better to have to work like a slave all one's life, than to face assault every time your old man came home drunk from the pub.

She rubbed clear a small patch of glass, slowly and cautiously. If anyone was inside, she didn't want them to see her. Her mouth opened silently as she stared at the two people. She couldn't tell who the man was, because his back was to the window, but she could see Eda Trott, shameless as you like, with not a stitch on.

Rea's eyes were riveted for a second or two. Then something caught her attention, and she craned her head sideways. She could have sworn she had seen a movement. Not on the bed, where passion was reaching its height, but low down on the floor. Not a rat or mouse, but something small and brightly coloured, bobbing along gently until it was within a few feet of the lovers.

Mere fear exploded into raging terror and Rea turned and fled. Her heart was banging so hard when she reached the house that she thought it was going to stop beating altogether. Up the back stairs and into the attic, door shut thankfully as she leaned against it, trembling.

Tottie May stirred, her voice bleary with sleep.

"Wass ... matter? What yer doin'?"

It was difficult to find enough saliva in her mouth to get words out, but Rea knew she must. Neither Tottie May, nor any other living person, must know what she had just seen. If the man knew she'd discovered them ... the man ...

"Nothin'. Just 'ad to ... well ... you know."

"Mm."

Tottie May fell back into slumber, hardly hearing the excuse as Rea clambered into bed and lay there shaking. At first, she hadn't known who the man was, and she still wasn't sure, but now she thought that there was something familiar about him.

She shut her eyes tightly, begging God to send her to sleep quickly. He probably wouldn't. God didn't listen much to the likes of her. One thing was certain though. No one must ever find out that she'd been there, or she'd die for sure. Mrs Trott mustn't guess; the man mustn't guess, and that thing which had jigged up to them ... that mustn't guess either.

She pulled the grubby sheet over her head, and for once in her life prayed that five o'clock would soon come.

After breakfast Marionette sent for Regina. She looked as
formidable as ever, stiffer and more lifeless than any of Louis's
puppets. She glanced over Regina's black merino gown, not
missing so much as an inch of the satin binding on the bodice and
perky little bustle, nor the real silver buttons down the front.

"Paris, of course, but why black?" she asked finally, when
Regina was seated. "Are you in mourning, or do you think it
flatters you?"

Regina adjusted her skirt, aware that Loveday Preece was
fussing away with the ornaments on the dressing-table, listening
to every word. She refused to be unnerved by Marionette. It was
high time she stood up to her, and dismissed the possibility that
she was anything more than a sick and temperamental woman
with a spiteful tongue.

"Yes, Paris, and I like black."

"So did I, when I was your age." Marionette's attention seemed
to wander. "Dear Lord, how long ago that seems. I could wear
white just as easily too, which is more than you could do with
that wishy-washy hair of yours."

"I do wear white, and no one has ever thought it ill-becoming
on me."

"Pleased with yourself, aren't you?" The piercing eyes were
concentrating again. "Young and lovely, you think the world's
at your feet, but it isn't, my dear. Oh no, indeed it isn't. Never
know what's round the corner. Just like me, on that day my
father and I set out for London."

Regina nodded, no longer doing battle.

"No, I know what you mean. I haven't said anything to you
since I came, Aunt Marionette, but ... but I'm sorry ... so very
sorry that ..."

"It's in the past. I don't want to talk about it. Tell me what
Paris is like nowadays?"

They spoke for a while about the French capital, and then of
the family. At eleven, Marionette sent Loveday off to get some
coffee.

"And what about the relations you've got here, eh? A fine lot,
aren't they?" She was scathing. "Louis a weakling, playing with

dolls; Marcelle man-mad; Victor a homosexual and worse, and Jeanne ..."

She broke off, and Regina said quickly:

"Jeanne is very troubled, you know. I tried to get her to write down what was upsetting her, but she wouldn't."

"Not your business."

"It's everyone's business when someone is as unhappy as Jeanne is. Her mother is hateful to her too. I'm sorry if I offend you, since Marcelle is your cousin, but she treats her daughter disgracefully."

"You don't offend me." Marionette's grimace was a real grin now. "There's nothing you can tell me about that woman which I don't know, but she's family. If I were up and about, things would be different."

"Couldn't you speak to her about Jeanne?"

"No." Flat and definite, the subject waved away with a flick of the hand. "Let it be."

But Regina couldn't, and she persisted.

"Perhaps it's the footsteps at night, or that strange singing. Either might be making Jeanne afraid."

The lids were closed, ignoring the words. It was as if Marionette were withdrawing herself from Regina. Finally, Regina got up and went to the window. She couldn't sit there any longer, feeling as if she were alone in the room, when all the time Marionette was there, a very real presence. She could see Tom Brody, an attractive boy of about seventeen, who had taken Dummer's place, working in the garden. He was clearing up leaves with a birch broom, and she watched the wind scatter them about and race across the tree-tops, making them rustle like taffeta being crunched up. There was one black crow on the sill, eyes bright and beady.

"Sit down." Marionette snapped her fingers. "Don't fidget, girl. What were you talking about just then? What footsteps?"

"I hear them at night."

"Nonsense."

"No it isn't, neither is that woman who sings. Who is she?"

"I've never heard anyone singing, nor walking about at night

either. It's your imagination. Best thing you can do is to get back
to France. You'll be saf ... happier there."

Regina was very still.

"You said safer."

"I said happier."

"But you meant ..."

"I know what I meant."

Marionette turned her head to look at Regina full in the face.
Regina could feel again the uncanny sensation, as if the room
were slipping by her, and she was moving towards the bed. She
braced herself, determined to fight it off, whatever it was, but it
didn't abate until Marionette looked away.

"Don't stay too long," she repeated quietly, and without
anger. "You've been warned. Who knows whether death has
finished with this house yet. Go home, girl, while you can."

Regina couldn't let it rest there. Marionette must be made to
speak more clearly, but there wasn't time. Loveday was back,
and with her was Vernon Morse, mouth thinner than ever,
cheeks as hollowed as a starving man's. But he wasn't starving.
His clothes were expensive, and the pomade he wore was costly.

Regina nodded to him, aware that he was ignoring her, gazing
past her to the bed. She saw the look Marionette and the doctor
exchanged, puzzled by it. Intimate? No, not that; not quite.
Secretive? No, not that either.

She shrugged as she left the room. There was a rapport
between them, yet quite what it was, she didn't know. It wasn't
her business, any more than Jeanne's problems were. It was just
one more small mystery, but Vernon Morse looked dangerous.

The rest of that day and the following night were uneventful.
Breakfast time came round again, with white linen table napkins
folded like mitres at each place, dishes of marmalade, jam, and
preserves in the centre, next to a whole honeycomb. Appetizing
smells were coming from the sideboard, where silver dishes
contained sizzling eggs, bacon, kidneys, fish, and mushrooms.

As Effie came in with the coffee, Regina was instantly

reminded of Louis's sketch. It really had been clever. Effie's puppet was exactly like the maid herself, down to the last strand of hair and fold of her apron. The tray was heavy, making Effie's arms slightly unsteady, giving her the same almost jerky appearance that the doll had had.

Regina took a hot roll, and forced the thought of the puppet out of her mind, and for a while there was silence as the family began the meal. Louis hardly bothered to eat, neither did Jeanne, but Victor and Denys had helped themselves liberally to the hot food, whilst Marcelle was positively stuffing herself with kidney, bacon and eggs.

When she had finished her third piece of toast and honey, Marcelle said sharply:

"You're slouching again, Jeanne! Sit up this minute. I should have thought Uncle Louis's opinion of you, which he expressed so clearly the other night, would have made you realise how ridiculous you seem to others." She cast Louis his share of her displeasure. "You look like a sack of potatoes."

Regina glanced at Philippe. He wasn't looking at Jeanne, but at Marcelle, and his expression was not pleasant.

"Do you hear me, Miss?" The temper was rising, along with Marcelle's colour. "Sit properly, or I'll take the strap to you."

Jeanne's face had been paper-white, shoulders bowed beneath the tirade and the humiliations piled on her, but the last words brought her to her feet, a string of loud and animal-like noises pouring from her as she rounded on her mother.

The others sat motionless, momentarily stunned by the turning of the worm. No one knew exactly what Jeanne was trying to say, but it wasn't difficult to guess. The blazing eyes and foam at the corners of the mouth told the story.

Then Jeanne leaned forward, picked up the honeycomb, and threw it straight at Marcelle. Marcelle screamed aloud as the sticky mess came into abrupt contact with her ample bosom, trickling down the foulard gown in a slow, yellowish rivulet.

"Never seen nothin' like it," said Effie, all agog, as she related the tale to Millie and the others in the kitchen. "Never thought she'd spit back like that, but 'er ma 'ad it comin'. Don't ever leave the poor lass alone for a minute. Cor, I thought I was goin' to burst out laughin' there and then."

"Good thing for you you didn't." Mrs Butcher was preparing a large steak and kidney pie. The pastry was on one side of the table, soft and floury; meat cut neatly on her left. "Well, go on. What 'appened then?"

"Well, Mr Pritchard and Master Vernon got the 'oney off 'er 'ighness, and she got up, red as a turkey-cock. Miss Regina was tryin' to quiet the girl, but she weren't listenin'. Just stood there, she did. You could see the rage run out of 'er, as if someone 'ad turned a tap on and poured it all away."

"Go on." Millie reached for her rolling pin. "What did 'er mother do then?"

"Nothin' at first. She was reel scared of 'er own daughter, and I can't say that I blames 'er. Miss Jeanne was like a madwoman. Even made me quake a bit, them noises she was makin'."

Rea was listening as she peeled potatoes, her back to the others. Jeanne a madwoman? Could that be anything to do with ...? She sniffed hard, cutting her finger as she jabbed a potato hard to force herself to pay attention to.the task in hand.

"She didn't say nothin'?" Mrs Butcher's violet eyes were on Effie's face. "Just kept quiet?"

"Only at first; till the shock wore off. Then she gave Miss Jeanne such a box round the ear that the girl nearly fell over. Would 'ave done, like as not, only that M. Lavisse caught 'er and steadied 'er." Effie paused, smiling slightly. "Ever so 'andsome, isn't 'e? Madame's cousin, I mean."

"Second cousin."

"If you say so, Mrs B. Anyways, 'e said something' to Mrs Pritchard what I couldn't catch, and then Miss Jeanne ran out of the room. Just like a crazy thing, she was."

Rea wished it was time to make the morning tea. She couldn't swallow properly, and the thoughts running round inside her head were making it pound. A good strong brew would put it right, but that wouldn't be for ages yet. A madwoman, Effie had said; like she was crazy.

"'Urry up with them potatoes, Rea," said Millie impatiently. "'Aven't got all day, you know, and when you've done them, put on the kettle. We'll 'ave our tea a bit earlier to-day, I think. Reckon we could send a cup up to Miss Jeanne, don't you? Steady 'er down a bit, maybe. You can take it to 'er, Rea."

Rea froze, but she knew it was no good arguing: she'd have to go. Up to the second floor, with a cup of tea for a madwoman.

Denys came out of the dressing-room and watched Marcelle putting the finishing touches to her toilette. She appeared to have got over the morning upset, for all her attention was on her eyelashes, which she was daubing with some black stuff which gave her the appearance of a loose woman. Pritchard's inward laugh was ironic.

Common or not, Noreen was as fresh as a daisy. She didn't need powder and paste and God knows what else to make her desirable, yet she was the whore, and Marcelle the wife. Quite a joke in a way.

He took another look at Marcelle. She was getting fatter, no doubt about that. Maybe her shoulders were still white, the flesh firm, but she was bulging now through stuffing herself with food and sweetmeats. Soon she'd be gross.

He shut his eyes, unable to stand the sight of her any longer. He'd have to get moving with his plan soon, or Noreen would send him packing, and that he couldn't let happen. However difficult and dangerous it would be to arrange, he'd have to do it, or lose Nor. Noreen, with her trim little body: not .thin, of course, but just nicely curved, with something in her which inflamed his mind to near madness.

He bit his lip. What made him think of madness? Then he knew. It was the scene at breakfast that morning. Jeanne, like a lunatic, mouthing what must have been obscenities at her mother, hating her, willing her dead, throwing that honey at her. It would have been funny, had it not been for the look in Jeanne's eyes. No cause for laughter there, and he'd been really shaken by it. Such a quiet, obedient child, or so he had thought. Put up with Marcelle's everlasting nagging without a murmur, until to-day. His frown deepened. Well, of course she'd had to put up with it without a murmur because she couldn't voice her protests, even if she'd wanted to.

Marcelle shouldn't have hit her like she did, no matter how provoked she was. Must have knocked the child half-silly, and Denys had almost shouted to Marcelle to stop. But he hadn't. He couldn't afford to quarrel with Marcelle just now, and besides, that man Lavisse seemed to have said all that was necessary. Couldn't catch the words, but Marcelle had lost her colour and sat down again as if someone had kicked her legs from under her. Serve her right, the old cow.

"You look very nice, ducks," he said, using the soft persuasive tone necessary to get money out of his wife. "Never seen a woman with neck and shoulders like yours. Pity we can't have your portrait painted. Good enough to save for posterity, you are."

Marcelle met his eyes in the mirror.

Damned fawning hypocrite. If he really thought her so attractive, why didn't he take advantage of her assets like a proper man, instead of going off to Kettle Street to that strumpet. He wanted money, of course, but she owed him one for getting found out the other night.

"No."

Blunt and positive, lips clamped together, as Pritchard's expression changed.

"Just a bit on loan, as it were?"

"Not a penny."

She didn't wait to argue any longer. She simply picked up her fan and swept out as if he didn't exist, and Pritchard saw the fury in himself in the looking glass.

Bitch! But perhaps it was a good thing. Noreen would have to wait for her ear-rings, but Marcelle's contempt was the spur he had needed. He'd waited long enough, being trampled underfoot by her. Now he'd do something, and quickly.

Whilst Marcelle had been putting on her evening face, Regina had been making her way upstairs to dress. She was nearing the landing from which the annexe stairs ran when the single gasolier went out. She gave a gasp, catching the banister rail.

It was remarkable enough that in such a well run house, the lights were always so few and far between. Odder still, that this one should go out of its own accord. She was trying to adjust her eyes to the blackness, when she caught a glimpse of a flickering light. It was moving about, a tiny glow in the darkness.

"Is anyone there?" Her voice was no steadier than her legs. "Who is it? Why have you turned the light out?"

She didn't expect an answer, and she didn't get one. All that happened was that the flame moved about again; first here, then there. She was about to call out for help, when the light came to rest, throwing itself on the five steps. It seemed brighter now, or perhaps another candle had been lit.

Her parched lips moved in disbelief when she saw it. A small Marcelle, some two foot high, complete with purple gown and pearls, moving slowly downstairs, nodding its head, one arm outstretched.

Regina screamed and put her hands over her eyes. The next thing she knew was that there were footsteps, lights had gone on, and someone was holding her tightly in his arms.

"Regina! In God's name, what is it?"

At last she dared to look up, seeing Philippe's face above her own, his hand still firmly about her waist. She moved her head, and saw the real Marcelle, large and wobbling in her purple gown; Pritchard smoothing his moustache with a nervous hand; Jeanne, eyes as wide as saucers; Effie, Rea, and Tottie May crowding in so that they didn't miss anything. Louis was there too, concerned and worried.

She told them haltingly what she had seen, and Lavisse said curtly:

"How absurd! You couldn't possibly have seen such a thing. Look for yourself; there's nothing on the stairs."

Every head turned with Regina's, contemplating the innocent carpet and brass stair-rods.

"Not now." She hoped Philippe wouldn't take his arm away too soon, for without its support she knew she would collapse and make an even bigger spectacle of herself than she had done already. "But it was there. I saw it! I really did!"

She begged Philippe with her eyes to believe her, but it was clear that he didn't. The hard mouth shewed no sympathy, and his look was almost inimical, yet the nearness of his body against hers still made her feel as she had never done before. Then he released her, and she was on her own to face the others.

"Really, Regina!" Marcelle was cross, for the screams had set her nerves jangling again. What with Jeanne behaving as she had done, and now this young and exquisite woman taking advantage of some female trick to get herself into Lavisse's arms ... it really was too much. "You ought to be ashamed of yourself. You have no thought for others; none at all. How could you have seen one of those marionettes? They're all in the workshop, you know that." She gave Louis a hard look. "Don't we all know it, seeing my own image was used so recently to make me into a figure of fun?"

Regina's hand tightened on the banister again, since this was now her only prop. Yes, Marcelle was right, the puppet should have been in the shed, but it wasn't. No matter how sceptical and disbelieving the others might be, she knew what she'd seen. The puppet had been there, coming downstairs by the light of a candle. Rea was right; the dolls were beginning to get into the house.

"It's my fault, all my fault." Louis took Regina's hand and squeezed it sympathetically. "I shouldn't have included that item in my show the other night. It's upset everyone, and I'm the one to be ashamed, but I meant no harm. Oh, my dear, I'm so sorry; truly sorry. You've been thinking about that scene, and it's preyed on your mind. I knew you were rather afraid of my children when you first saw them, and I should have known better than to ..."

"No!" She had to stop the flow of Louis's chatter and remorse. "No, Uncle Louis, it was nothing to do with that. I saw a marionette on the stairs just now, the one which looks like Marcelle. I don't care whether you think I'm imagining it, or mischief-making, or even going mad. I know I'm not. The thing was there, and I saw it. Forgive me, I can't come down to dinner to-night."

She left them standing there, mounting the stairs and closing her door firmly behind her, the tears oozing out from under her lashes. She had meant what she said: she didn't care what anyone else thought. A drop of moisture fell on to her hand. Well, perhaps that wasn't quite true. She cared what Philippe thought, and what he had thought was obvious.

He had been the first to reach her. Could he have contrived to … no … that wasn't possible. Yet he was the son of a puppeteer, if he really was Lavisse. He could … She drew a deep breath. No, Philippe hadn't been there; no one had. It had been just the doll, gliding down the steps, one hand held out as if it were about to take her own.

Loveday Preece finished dressing Marionette's hair and put the brush aside to be washed. Madame was very particular. Every brush and comb had to be thoroughly cleansed in soapy water each morning. Loveday didn't mind. She was proud of her mistress's fastidiousness, and in any event it wasn't her place to dispute orders, particularly orders from Mme. Boussard.

She re-arranged the willows, setting one or two branches straight, and then moved all the silver ornaments from the mantelpiece so that she could brush the velvet with which it was draped. The other servants were only allowed in here to bring food. Loveday looked after the room, as she looked after the woman in the bed, and the collection of priceless jewellery which was kept in the tallboy.

Once, there had been companions, but they hadn't lasted long. Loveday's grin was self-satisfied. They'd soon gone, and now only she was left to care for madame. It was a privilege she guarded jealously.

Marionette was looking at her reflection in a hand mirror, baring her teeth.

"It grows no better with the years, does it?"

"Pardon, madame?"

"No matter." Wearily Marionette laid the glass down, leaning back against the fresh pillow cases. Clean bed-linen every day; blankets changed twice a week. A washerwoman came in to help with the mountain of laundry, for the maids couldn't cope with it alone. "Loveday."

"Yes, madame?"

"I think it may be soon."

The heavily-set woman turned from the fireplace to look at her mistress, alert as she nodded.

"Will it?"

"I believe so."

Preece inclined her head again. She never questioned Marionette Boussard's words or her judgment. With powers such as the mistress had, it would be folly to do so. Just listen and obey; that was all which was required.

"The question is …"

Loveday waited silently, seeing that Marionette was really talking to herself, not daring to break into the inner secrets which weren't for her to know.

"The question is, Loveday, can I stop it, before it stops me?"

She saw the awe on her servant's face, and half-smiled.

"You don't know, do you, and neither do I, but that's the question. Will I win, or will …?"

"Oh yes!" Preece was fervent in her assurance. "Yes, yes, madame, you'll win. You always do."

Seven

"Don't care what anyone else thinks, Miss," said Rea, as she put Regina's early morning tea on the bedside table. "Supposed to leave this outside, but I thought I'd bring it in to-day, 'cos I wanted to tells you I believes you, no matter what."

"Thank you, Rea."

Regina sat up and pulled the bedclothes straight, whilst Rea made up the fire. Regina had kept it alight all night, sitting beside it until nearly four o'clock, unable to face bed and darkness.

"Yes." The kitchenmaid came back to Regina's side, her face pasty beneath a smudge or two of soot. It wasn't her job to take tea round really, but Tottie May was idle and spiteful too; it wasn't wise to fall out with her. Better yet another chore, and a hundred more steps, than a quarrel or worse. "I know what missus can do. Struck Miss Jeanne dumb three years ago, she did. No one knows what Miss Jeanne did to upset 'er, but she never spoke no more after that."

"She was ill." Regina wouldn't let herself be drawn into such a discussion. Her recollection of the happenings of the previous evening was still too clear. "That was the fever, nothing to do with Mme. Boussard."

"Oh yes it were, and now you've seen ... that ... that thing what looks like Mrs P., I reckon she's in trouble too. She'll be next, you see." The girl looked at Regina silently for a second or two, rubbing one foot against the other leg. "Them things are gettin' bolder, ain't they? Comin' into the 'ouse just as they please. Sometimes I wonder if it's just 'er what makes 'em come, or whether they ..."

Regina couldn't resist it.

"What things?"

Rea didn't reply, but she didn't have to. Regina knew the answer without the need for words.

"And that's not all." Rea leaned forward confidentially. "I only 'eard meself yesterday. Mrs Butcher was talkin' to Effie, see, but they didn't know I was there."

"You shouldn't listen to other people's conversations. It's not the right thing to do."

Rea took the comment in the spirit in which it was given; a mild, conventional rebuke. Then she went on with her tale, which Regina was as anxious to hear as Rea was to relate it.

"It seems there was another girl what died, a long time ago."

"Another!" The delicate brows came sharply together. "You must be mistaken."

"No, that's what Mrs B. said. She weren't 'ere at the time, o' course, but you know 'ow these things get about. There was another one. It was like this ..."

She bent closer still, whispering eagerly until Regina's face was the colour of the sheet. Then she picked up the empty cup and scuttled off, leaving Regina to lean back and close her eyes as she tried to forget what she had just heard.

By that afternoon, Regina had pulled herself together, ashamed that she had let nerves get the better of her. More ashamed still that others had seen her weakness, particularly Philippe Lavisse.

Rea's tale of a girl's death long ago was dismissed. There was nothing mysterious about it; it was a question of cause and effect. Young women in circumstances like that often died; it was regrettable, but true.

Regina was also determined to put the dolls firmly in their place. She had let the sight of them undermine her good sense until she had imagined they could move of their own free will or be manipulated by Marionette from afar. It was not like her to be so fanciful. Wax heads, bits of wood, scraps of material, daubs of paint. They didn't come into the house by themselves, nor did Marionette summon them in.

She clung to her new-found determination as she went into the sitting-room at four o'clock. Philippe was there, but no one else seemed to be about. He rose politely, but she had the feeling he was not glad to see her, and sighed in relief when Effie appeared with a large tray. It would give her hands something to do. There was a silver kettle hanging over a small spirit lamp, fluted tea pot, milk-jug and sugar bowl, with cups and saucers of finest porcelain. In a few minutes Effie was back with a stand containing wafer thin sandwiches, biscuits, and sugared cakes.

When Effie had finally gone and Regina had started to pour, she said casually:

"I'm sorry I was stupid last night. What must you have thought of me?"

"That you should follow the example of the Misses Brontë, and put such tales on paper. You would be highly rewarded, I'm sure."

She was proud that her hand didn't shake as she passed his cup.

"That is a thought, of course. Make fiction out of fact."

She hadn't meant to say that. All her good intentions about being sensible and not allowing her imagination to run riot were gone again as he raised his head and gave her a steady look.

"You still persist in your story?"

"It wasn't a story. I saw that puppet, as clearly as I am seeing you now." She took a much needed sip of her own tea. How could she have thought she could dismiss the small Marcelle, even for a minute? "Philippe, haven't you noticed something about this house? Does it seem quite normal to you?"

"Perfectly."

He was being deliberately unhelpful, leaving the burden of her doubts entirely on her own shoulders.

"I don't think it is. I noticed something wrong as soon as I arrived. I don't know what it was exactly. It's difficult to put it into words, but ..."

"You must try, if you're going to be a novelist."

"Philippe!" Anger lent her spirit. "Please do not make fun of me. I'm serious."

"So you are." The hooded lids were half-down. "How very

extraordinary, but do go on. You thought there was something wrong when you first arrived, and ...?"

"Well, there have been these peculiar occurrences, haven't there? First, the maid who fell downstairs, and then the two companions who vanished. Even since we've been here, Herr Von Heltz and Caleb Dummer have died." She hesitated. "Also, Rea told me to-day that there was another girl who died, a long time ago."

He refused the sandwiches she was offering him and sighed.

"My dear Regina, the first servant pitched down a dangerous flight of iron steps in the half-light; it could have happened to anyone. The two companions couldn't stand Marionette any longer and walked out, and I don't blame them. She's selfish, ill-tempered, and probably made their lives hell. Von Heltz dropped asleep whilst he was smoking in bed, and a pile of stones slipped and fell on Dummer. There is nothing sinister about any' of these things. If there had been, the police would have been much more interested."

"But the girl who died long ago ..."

"What a one you are for listening to servants' gossip. May I have another cup of tea please? My mother says that servants seldom tell the whole truth, for they never recognise it when they hear it, and that their greatest enemy is not hard work, hunger, or cold, but boredom. They have no lives of their own, so they make things up to lighten the tedium."

"I thought that at first, but not now."

Lavisse watched her near despair, keeping his eyes half-closed so that there would be no danger of her reading his thoughts. She was the most beautiful thing he had ever seen, and in that brief time when he had held her in his arms, his emotions, normally tightly under control, had taken a battering. But lovely or not, he had come to Chantry Close for a purpose, and he couldn't allow this enchanting creature to get in his way. He said coolly:

"I think you ask too many questions about things which aren't your concern. Isn't it time you went home? You said you were only staying for a few days. Why are you still here?"

Regina knew that she looked guilty; knew also that he would

spot it. She should have gone, of course, but whilst Philippe was here she couldn't bring herself to leave, even though fear was mounting inch by inch.

"You are so anxious to be rid of me." She was moving the sugar bowl a fraction to the left, frightened of what her hands would do if left unoccupied. "I wonder why."

Their eyes met suddenly, and she felt as if he were pinning her to the chair. The light was almost gone, and Effie hadn't come back yet to deal with the gasoliers. Only the fire illuminated Lavisse's face, but the red glow didn't warm its contours. He was as cold as ice.

"No reason." He shrugged. "I just think you'd be better back in Paris. You are too inquisitive, and you know what happens to cats with curiosity."

"I am not a cat," she retorted, "and why do you walk about the house late at night?"

"More questions?" The voice was very soft, but the tone was like steel. "It is not your business, but since you are so interested in what I do, I will tell you. I have been up to town once or twice, and have come home very late. Does that satisfy you, or would you like me ot be more specific as to what I do in the Haymarket?"

She flushed, the reprimand for her impertinence hurting, but not as much as the reason for Lavisse's trips. If he went to London, to the Haymarket, late in the evening, it could only be for one purpose. She forced tears back, thankful now that the lights weren't on.

"I see, but now and then I've seen you in your dressing-room. You were in the passage that night."

"You are wrong." He was colder still. "I have already said that whoever you saw on that occasion, it was not me. But let me give you some advice, Regina, and pay heed to it. It follows that if you see people walking about when they should be in bed, you too are up and prowling. Stop it, before it's too late."

Her colour fled.

"Too late? What do you mean?"

"What I say. Who knows what might happen to you if you

don't keep your nose out of other people's business? You've been warned."

His smile was a threat, and her alarm leapt another degree. Did Philippe mean that she had been warned by what he had just said, or could he have been referring to some incident which had already taken place. Her mind flew to the attic, and to that paralysing moment when someone had slipped a hand into the opening of her robe. Philippe? Oh God, not Philippe!

"May I light the gasoliers, Miss?"

Regina almost gasped as Effie appeared in the doorway, not daring to risk pouring another cup of tea in case it rattled in her hand.

"Of course."

She sounded breathless, even to herself, but Philippe was very calm.

"Yes, Regina, I do so agree with you. That particular self-portrait of Rembrandt is a masterpiece. How I would like to add it to my own collection."

It was cold inside the workshop, and Regina was shivering. Louis had an iron basket, punched with holes, containing coal and wood, but it wasn't helping much. She hadn't wanted to set foot in the place again, but when Louis had asked her after breakfast if she would go with him to see the mask he had made of Lavisse's face, she couldn't resist the wistfulness in him.

She was glad that they were in the part of the building where the work was done. At least she couldn't see them from here. They were safely tucked away behind the curtains, but, even so, the very thought of them made new chills run through her.

"I always begin this way," Louis was saying as carefully he began to remove the white cloth. "I model the head and face from this, you see. Well, what do you think of it?"

Regina's lips parted, but for a second or two she couldn't speak. The wax impression looked like the face of a cadaver. It was just as if she were staring down at Lavisse after death, and it took every ounce of strength in her to steady herself.

"It's marvellous. So like Philippe."

He was pleased, wrapping the mask up again with pride.

"Yes, I think so too. I shall start making the puppet to-night."

Another marionette! Inside the muff, her fingers were locked together. A puppet which looked like Philippe. She was going to plead that she was cold as an excuse to return to the house, when she caught a flash of colour out of the corner of her eye, her head turning abruptly. There on the shelf was a marionette. It wasn't hanging up, but propped against the wall as if it were sitting down for a rest.

She went on staring at it. It looked as if it had just stepped off the stage of La Scala, Milan. A prima donna; deep chested, olive skin, shining black hair drawn back into a bun; elaborately embroidered gown, sparkling jewels, and sloe eyes which winked in the light of the lantern.

"Uncle." She whispered it, in case the doll could hear her. "Who ... what is that?"

He glanced up, finished with the mask, and gave a happy smile.

"Oh, that's my darling Marta Rosa; my little opera singer. She's one of my best efforts. Even her jaw has been made to move, so it really appears that she is singing."

"Marta Rosa?"

"Yes, that's right. Do you know, it's the strangest thing. I couldn't find her for at least two weeks or more. I know I left her with the others, but somehow she disappeared. I was really worried and searched everywhere, and then, only this morning, I found her here again. I'm so glad to have her back: she's beautiful, isn't she?"

His voice was low and loving as he reached out for the marionette.

"Every detail is accurate, you know. It took me a long time to make her, for I wanted her to be perfect. One half expects her to begin an aria at any moment, don't you think?"

"Yes." Regina tried not to back away, but the slivers of black glass seemed to be fixed on her. "Yes, she's ... she's very lovely. Uncle Louis."

"Yes, my dear?" He wasn't really paying attention to Regina, more concerned with replacing the marionette comfortably on the shelf. "What is it?"

"Have you heard someone singing in the house lately?"

"Singing?" He looked round in surprise. "Why no, I don't think so. You mean one of the servants?"

"No, no, not them. It's nearly always at night. A woman who sings a song I've never heard before. It's ... well ... haunting."

"Oh, at night." Louis didn't seem aware of her white face or the quaver in her voice. "No, I sleep very soundly, so I wouldn't hear anything once I'm in bed. Are you sure, Regina?"

"Yes, I'm sure. The servants have heard it too, but please don't tell anyone I said that, because they're afraid Aunt Marionette will dismiss them if she knows they've said such things."

"I won't say a word," he promised solemnly, "but I think maybe they're playing on your imagination. I don't mean they're making fun of you, or anything like that, but they dearly love something different to talk about."

"I don't think it's that at all. They seemed genuinely frightened."

"I shouldn't worry about them." He laughed gently. "Any emotion is better than none, even fear. Now and then I wonder what it must be like to be a servant. No life of one's own; always at the beck and call of others. Basement, attic, work. What do they see of life?" He turned to stroke the doll's skirt. "Perhaps it was Marta Rosa trying to scare them. She's a naughty girl, you know."

He took her arm, leading her to the door.

"And you think I've caught Philippe well?"

"Yes, indeed."

She forced herself to listen to him, because she couldn't dwell on what else he'd just said. Perhaps it was Marta Rosa? The doll who had been missing for more than two weeks. The tiny prima donna who had mysteriously returned to her rightful place. The singing was in the house; had Marta Rosa been there too?

"Yes, uncle." She quailed as the door closed behind them, keeping the conversation going at all cost. "It's a fine piece of work. Where did you learn mask making?"

"In France. I was apprenticed to a man who made waxworks

and masks. He taught me a lot. Some of what I learned has been most useful to me in my hobby here."

They walked up the garden, light snow falling on them and clinging to Regina's lashes.

"That photograph by Aunt Marionette's bed."

"Mm?"

Louis turned his collar up, keeping hold of her arm to steady her on the slippery ground.

"Who is it?"

"Oh, just someone my dear wife knew years ago." He was smiling slightly as they reached the side door. "A long long time ago."

Regina could see the sadness in the smile as they shut the wind and snow out, moving on into the hall. It was obvious that Louis still cared deeply for Marionette, yet she kept the photograph of another man by her bed. Despite Lavisse's admonition to stop asking questions, she said tentatively:

"Don't you mind? About the photograph, I mean."

He shook his head, the corners of his mouth still lifted in artificial amusement, as if he were trying not to remember too deeply.

"No, I don't mind. She hasn't got much, has she, and a photograph can't hurt anyone."

She said nothing more as he handed his coat to Tottie May, who had appeared from behind the green baize door, apologising because Effie was not there to relieve him of his outer garments. Louis obviously didn't consider the respective duties of the maids to be of any importance, or else he was still thinking of the photograph, for he merely gave the girl a vague nod and went off to his study.

"Cold out, ain't it, Miss?"

"Very. Tottie May, have you heard that singing recently?"

Tottie May was evasive as she moved towards the door leading to the basement.

"No, I 'aven't. Rea says we won't no more. Gone away, so she told Effie last night, though 'ow she knows so much, I'm sure I can't think. Is that all, Miss?"

"Yes thank you."

Regina's voice was faint, and for a moment she couldn't face the stairs. The singing had stopped, so Rea said. Marta Rosa was back in the workshop.

"Well, and what have you been doing to-day?"

Marionette seemed less hostile that evening when Regina went to say good-night. She had a gossamer thin shawl about her shoulders, half a dozen valuable rings on her fingers, contriving to look like a queen holding court.

"Nothing very much." Regina sat down by the bed, wondering if Marionette were going to criticize the white taffeta gown trimmed with handmade lace. "Oh, I did go to the workshop this morning. Uncle Louis has made a mask of Philippe's face. He says he always does this when he is going to make a puppet in the likeness of someone."

She watched Marionette's reaction closely. The dark eyes gave nothing away; even the fingers betrayed no reaction, slack on the counterpane.

"Yes, I believe he does. I was wrong; you can wear white. A charming dress."

It was the first compliment Regina had received from Marionette, but she was not going to be deflected as she murmured her thanks.

"It was very like Philippe, except ... that ... that it looked as though he were dead."

This time there was a flicker behind the lowered eyelashes; the fingers twitched almost imperceptibly. Regina pressed the advantage.

"Uncle Louis said he was apprenticed to a man who made waxworks and masks."

"Yes."

"Did you know the man?"

"Yes." Mme. Boussard was rather white round the mouth, not looking at Regina. "I knew him. He was very clever. His death-masks were famous."

Then Marionette waved a curt dismissal, and somewhat

shaken, Regina found herself outside on the landing. Death-masks? Philippe? She told herself she was being stupid again. That was the way Uncle Louis always worked; he'd said so.

"Cross, was she?"

Regina hadn't heard Loveday Preece until she was almost at her elbow, and smothered a startled exclamation, but the woman made no apology.

"Cross?" Regina took a deep breath. "No, I don't think so."

Regina didn't know why she was bothering to answer the insolent question of a mere servant, but there was something about Loveday Preece that made it difficult to ignore her. There was a force in her, but what kind Regina didn't care to dwell on.

"No, my aunt seems in a perfectly good humour."

"Well she ain't, I can tell you." Preece looked at Regina scornfully, as if she thought her a fool. "Just found out that Mrs P. 'as another lover, and she's that jealous. Missus can't ever 'ave lovers no more, you see. 'Asn't been able to 'ave 'em for years; not since the accident. Can't forgive those what enjoy such pleasures."

Regina drew herself up. It was time to stop this, however formidable the woman might seem.

"That is gossip, Preece, and it is ill-becoming to speak of your mistress so. Good-night."

The cackle followed her upstairs, where she found Rea making up the fire for the last time that night.

"Should stay alight till early hours." Rea brushed the dust neatly away and stood up. "Must keep out the chill, Miss."

"Yes."

Rea looked thinner than ever, cheeks almost as sunken as Vernon Morse's, yet Regina was sure Millie Butcher wouldn't keep the child short of food.

"Are you all right, Rea? You look …"

Fear nipped the corners of the kitchenmaid's mouth, her hand shaking on the handle of the brass scuttle.

"Yes, Miss."

"You'd tell me if anything was wrong, wouldn't you? I migh` be able to help."

"Nothin' wrong." Rea moved sideways like a crab to the door. "Nothin' at all."

"She's gone, hasn't she?"

Rea's eyes widened, her flight stopped momentarily.

"She?"

"Marta Rosa." Regina' voice was very quiet. "She's left the house, hasn't she?"

Rea's lower lip quivered.

"Don't know what you mean, Miss. Must go."

Regina stared at the closed door. Rea was too petrified to discuss the matter but, of course, the whole thing was a fairy tale anyway. She told herself that several times as she undressed and got into bed. She had broken the promise she'd made to herself to be sensible, and let herself be swept along on a tide of tittle-tattle and ignorant superstition.

To divert her thoughts, she turned to Marcelle. A new lover? Someone else coming to the side door? Well, it wasn't her business, as Lavisse had said most emphatically.

The clock was wound, the candle snuffed out; nothing but the comforting flicker of the fire playing on the ceiling. The featherbed was soft and seductive; sleep was very near as her eyes began to close.

The dream, when it came, was horrible. A place which seemed familiar, with someone hiding in the shadows in the corner. Then Marta Rosa, life size now, heaving bosom and flashing eyes as she sang louder and louder. Then, whatever it was in the corner began to move, and Regina fought to awaken herself before it could touch her.

"No!"

She sat upright, aroused at last and trembling, just in time to hear a door close somewhere. The side door? It was a long way away, yet the sound had been clear enough. Marcelle going to her new lover, or just part of the dream?

Regina turned on her side and fell asleep again, thinking of Philippe Lavisse.

A short time before, Marcelle Pritchard had been alone in her bedroom. Denys had gone out as usual, off to Kettle Street, no doubt, although he had made the usual excuse about a concert. Silly fool. Did he really imagine anyone in Chantry Place believed him?

She frowned as there was a tap on the door.

"Yes, who is it?"

"Me, mother; Victor."

She smiled at him lovingly as he came up to the dressing-table. He really was a fine boy; so like her to look at. All that nonsense she'd gleaned from the servants about him and Von Heltz must have been untrue, like most of what those idle girls below had to say. Yet Marcelle was not sorry that the German was gone. Not glad that he'd died the way he had, of course, but glad he was no longer there to tempt a susceptible boy.

"Yes, darling, what is it?"

He was patently embarrassed, not knowing how to begin, and she laughed.

"Come, love, tell me. What is it?"

"I need some money, mother."

The pale blue eyes considered Victor's face carefully. He looked desperate; not like a lad asking for pocket money, but a man almost in agony.

"Oh?" She turned back to the mirror, concentrating on her hair. "What for?"

"Just some things I've got to buy."

"You've got your allowance."

"It's all gone."

It was on the tip of her tongue to ask whether he'd given it to Conrad, but she decided against it. She wouldn't ask him if there was someone who had taken the German's place either, although she'd seen Victor watching the new gardener more than once. It was a subject she wanted to push down into the depths of her mind, clinging to the conviction that it was merely servants' talk which branded her son as some kind of pervert.

"Well, you'll have more in two weeks' time."

"I can't wait, and it won't be enough anyway."

The brush paused in mid-air.

"Not enough? My dear, what can you want that is so expensive?"

"I can't tell you. May I have some money?"

"Sweetheart, I haven't got any." Her gaze was limpid. "You know I'd give you anything I had, but Marionette keeps me short too." There was a note of acid in her voice. "She could double my allowance and never notice it, but she won't."

"I've got to have some!" Victor was red in the face, thrusting out his chin. "Don't you understand? I've got to have it, now!"

He was exasperated with her for not realising how vital it was. He'd taken to Tom at once, and Tom had responded, but the young gardener was as demanding as Conrad had been. After their first encounter, the hints began. Later they became more than hints, and Victor had to satisfy Tom somehow.

"Don't get excited, it's bad for you." Marcelle turned to him again, startled when she saw the perspiration on his forehead and something behind his eyes she'd never seen before. It was that gardener, after all. He'd have to go, like Jacob. She would speak to Louis in the morning. "You'll have to wait, Victor."

"I can't, I tell you, I can't! You've got some put away; I know you have."

Marcelle's nostrils were pinched, her voice hard and flat.

"That's not true."

"Yes it is! You're a mean old pig, and I wish you were dead!"

"Victor! How dare you? If I tell you I haven't got money, then I haven't. Now go to bed. It's very late, and never speak to me like that again."

"Perhaps I'll never have to speak to you in any way, ever again."

He flounced out of the room, slamming the door behind him. When he was gone, Marcelle got up and lifted down the small oil-painting by the bureau, turning it round and removing the package taped to the back. Quickly she counted the bank notes, her flush deepening with fury. Someone had taken at least ten pounds. It had to be either Victor or Denys. Victor had said he knew she had money, but had he guessed where it was? Had

Denys found out, and robbed her in order to ply his trollop with gifts?

Marcelle put the painting back and sat down by the dressing-table. To-morrow she'd find out who had had the effrontery to steal from her, and then God help them. She'd also deal with Victor's new friend too, in no uncertain manner.

Meanwhile, she mustn't let herself get upset, or she wouldn't enjoy what lay ahead, and opportunities like this were too good to waste.

A touch more powder; the neck of the robe opened a bit more to reveal lace and milky flesh; heavy perfume behind the ears and on the throat.

Denys would be gone for hours, so she needn't worry about him. Nothing to think about now but desire. Her ire forgotten, she took her candle and left her room, quietly going downstairs and along the side passage. She hardly noticed the cold, for her excitement was growing. She knew he'd be waiting, for he'd promised, and he never broke his word.

She paused once by the side door, frowning. Had that been a noise? The candle was lifted up, but there was nothing to be seen except what looked like a brightly coloured handkerchief under a table by the wall. She paid it no heed. One of the servants would pick it up when they cleaned in the morning.

She smoothed the doubt away, smiling as she turned the knob and opened the door. He was there. She couldn't see his face, but his hand was firm on hers, and her pulse quickened.

When the door slammed loudly behind her in the wind, she hesitated, fearing someone might have heard it, but the man was pulling her after him. What did it matter anyway? Let them hear. She didn't care a damn.

Eight

They found Marcelle the next morning. Tom Brody was the first to see her, hanging limp from the branch of a tree, her toes dangling only a few inches from the ground. He stared transfixed at the bloated face, the horror creeping up from his feet like a deadly tide as he saw the puppet next to her. A puppet which looked exactly like her, with a string round its neck.

The family and servants answered his hoarse cries at once, stunned as they regarded Marcelle and her tiny replica.

"Dear God!"

Louis's voice was a quaver, the others silent in the face of tragedy.

"Why did she do it?"

Lavisse looked at Boussard quickly.

"You think it was suicide?"

"What else could it be? No one would want to hurt Marcelle."

Regina was ashen, too shaken to notice the biting wind; oblivious to the ring of upturned faces.

Victor coughed, covering his fear. He'd never realised before how old his mother was, but now that life was extinct, it was obvious enough. She had been ageing and mean; almost as mean as Marionette. She could well have afforded to give him a few pounds, but she'd pretended she hadn't any. Now it would be easier. She was dead, and he knew where she'd hidden her notes.

Jeanne was exulting silently, although her face gave nothing away. She'd never again have to listen to that shrill, nagging voice exhorting her to sit up. Never again would she be made to look stupid in front of others; never again would Marcelle's heavy hand fall on her as if she were a child of six. It was her moment of triumph, and she wanted to shout with joy, regretting more than ever before that she couldn't utter a word. If she could have spoken, she would have told the others how richly her mother had deserved to die.

Pritchard was trembling. The sight of his wife's heavy body and her wide open eyes made him want to vomit. Heaven knows he'd been tired of her and her spiteful jibes and parsimonious habits. True, he planned ... No! This wasn't the time to remember the plans. Things were going well, but it was just that she looked so helpless, now that she was dead. In life, Marcelle had never been helpless.

"Get the police," said Lavisse to Brody, whose delicate skin and gold curls made him look like a pretty girl. "There's nothing for you to be frightened about; just get off to the station as quickly as you can."

He watched the boy's unsteady gait, then said shortly:

"The rest of you come inside. There's nothing to be done here." He motioned the servants to hurry, ignoring their tears and wails. "Come along, before you all get pneumonia."

Regina didn't move; she was still looking at Marcelle.

"How did she do it?"

Lavisse was brisk.

"Simple enough. She had a rope, and there's a box just over there which she must have stood on, and then kicked it away from under her."

"But ... but that thing next to her. How did it get there?"

Philippe was herding them indoors, pulling Regina along by her hand.

"I've no idea, unless she put it there herself."

They went into the sitting-room, smaller and more comfortable than the spacious drawing-room with its dove grey curtains and a Persian carpet so valuable that it almost forbade anyone to step on its surface.

It was whilst they were getting warm and drinking tea laced with rum, that Jeanne came up to Lavisse with a folded paper in her hand. Regina hadn't noticed that the girl had gone, but she must have slipped away, for when Philippe asked if the note had been in Marcelle's bedroom, Jeanne nodded.

Brody had gone for the police, as instructed, but they wouldn't be there for another ten minutes or more, and grimly Lavisse opened the note and read it. His voice was very quiet, yet the room was so silent that no one missed a single syllable of what Marcelle had written.

"She says she is going to take her life, because her one true love has tired of her, and there is nothing worth living for now."

Pritchard cleared his throat nervously, fiddling with his tie-pin.

"Who was the man? Does she say?"

"No, simply that he came to the side door to fetch her now and then. It could have been anyone."

Regina swallowed convulsively. That side door once more.

Louis was touching his eyes with his handkerchief, overcome.

"Poor woman, poor woman, how she must have suffered."

"Well, perhaps, but ..."

"Don't judge her, Philippe." Louis's voice was low. "It's not easy being deeply in love, you know, especially when that love isn't returned."

Regina knew what he was thinking, and said hastily:

"And he came to fetch her at the side door? The servants whispered about that door, and now I can see why."

Lavisse was curt.

"That's enough, Regina, don't make matters worse."

She shrank back from his anger, but her heart grew heavier. Could Marcelle's 'true love' have been Philippe after all, as she had once thought? Philippe claimed that he had only just arrived in England, but who was to say that he was speaking the truth. He could easily have been staying in London, perhaps living quite near to Chantry Close, so that he could visit Marcelle when he wanted to. Perhaps they'd grown tired of being apart, and so Philippe had suddenly appeared as a relation of Marionette's, thus making easier their liaison.

She had always thought there was something wrong with

Lavisse's claim that he was Marionette's second cousin, yet could Philippe really have craved for that thing which had just been found outside in the garden? She'd dismissed the idea earlier because she couldn't bear the thought of it, but such cases were not unknown. Her mother had told her of a man, even younger than Philippe, who had been madly in love with a woman of sixty, and not simply because she had been rich. The human heart was never predictable. But, if it hadn't been Lavisse, then, as he himself had said, they would never know who her paramour had been.

"What does she say about the marionette?" Regina forced herself to stop thinking of Marcelle in Philippe's arms. "Did she put it there?"

Philippe's lips were a thin straight line.

"I don't know. She doesn't mention it."

"Then perhaps ..."

"Yes?"

Regina was aware that she was the target of every eye, and she knew that they had all guessed what she was about to say. She could feel waves emanating from them, daring her to upset the neat answer which Marcelle's note had provided, and in the end she couldn't finish her sentence.

"Nothing... it's nothing."

The police stayed longer that time, but eventually they reached the same conclusion as Louis had done. Marcelle Pritchard had been rejected by some unknown man, and had done away with herself. What more was there to say?

Regina longed to ask Inspector Brewster what he had made of the marionette, but when she looked out of the window, watching his men lower the body to the ground, she saw the doll had gone. If she mentioned it now, Brewster would think her crazy, and Lavisse would be furious with her for making trouble. But who had removed the puppet?

She went up to her room where she could be alone, chilled by her thoughts. She ought to leave. It was time to go now, before it was too late, as Marionette had said. Yet something still held her back. She had no reason to doubt Marcelle's sad message, for

Denys, Victor and Mrs Butcher had all confirmed that it was in the dead woman's handwriting, yet the doubt was there all the same. Why hadn't the puppet still been there when the police arrived?

A suicide would not stop to tie her likeness to the branch of the tree on which she proposed to hang herself, particularly Marcelle who had no time for the dolls. A dead woman couldn't remove the doll either. Regina forced herself back to sanity. Maybe one of the policemen had simply cut it down thinking it of no importance.

But if Marcelle had not killed herself, then somebody else had done so.

Vernon Morse stood for a long while looking at the tree branch, a faint smile on his thin lips. He'd been called to tend Mme. Boussard, simply as a matter of form, for she needed no help from him. Pity Marcelle had been such a fool. Not a bad looking woman at all: a good, round figure, with plenty of flesh, just as he liked the female form to be. But she'd been stupid; very stupid. The sharp breeze ruffled the dark waves, making them untidy. He sighed, putting his top hat on again and turning away. Ah well. Perhaps it was for the best, after all.

At tea-time the staff gathered round the comfort of the range. Once a month, always on a Thursday, Millie got them all hot muffins, purchased from the man who walked round the streets ringing his bell. They were large and spongy, melting in the mouth, and on every occasion Millie said the same thing.

"Nice to eat somethin' I 'aven't cooked meself. A reel change."

They nodded, wiping oozing butter from their chins. Muffins were never served at the white wood table like ordinary meals. Muffin day was special, and they huddled round the stove, drinking strong brown tea and chattering in between mouthfuls.

It was still bitter outside, but the floral curtains had been pulled over the windows and several oil-lamps were alight, winking on brass and copper. It was cosy and safe, and they had a really worth while topic of conversation this time.

"Reckon she did it 'erself, don't you?"

"'Course she did, Effie." Millie was spreading butter thickly. No sense in spoiling the ship for a ha'porth of tar. "Wrote that letter and said so, didn't she?"

"Yes, but maybe she was made to do it."

Tottie May swallowed the last delicious morsel of her third muffin and reached for another.

"What d'yer mean, made to do it?"

"By missus, of course, 'oo else?"

Millie shot a look at Rea, utterly silent, her delicacy untouched. That child was getting thinner by the day. Losing weight, and so pale that she was like a little ghost. Millie had watched her for some time now. Not eating any more, or not much anyway. Never knew a skivvy before who wasn't ravenous, ready to tuck into the heavy suet puddings and boiled meat pies which were Mrs Butcher's speciality.

"Don't you like it, Rea?"

Rea started, flushing uncomfortably.

"Oh yes, Mrs Butcher, it's ever so nice."

"Then eat it, girl, it'll put some flesh on your bones. 'Ere, 'ave a bit more butter."

She knew Rea wasn't going to obey, but she turned back to Effie. She'd done her best. Whatever was wrong with the child would come out in the end. Looked very much like a young sister of her own, who'd died of tuberculosis. Maybe that was it. Time would tell.

"You mean madame forced 'er to take 'er life?"

"Not in so many words, but ... well ... you know."

Tottie May nodded and so did Mrs Butcher. They both understood.

"More, Effie? Plenty left. Tottie May, another cuppa tea, if you'd be so kind."

Everyone was very polite on treat days; even Millie didn't issue orders as she normally did. It was an hour unlike any other in the month. Almost like a small holiday.

"'Ere you are, Mrs B. 'Ot and sweet, as you likes it."

"Thank you, Tottie May. Well, what can we do about it?"

"Nothin'." Effie was emphatic. "You knows well enough we daresn't try to interfere. If we did, she'd 'ave us too."

Rea bit back a cry, and Millie said chidingly:

"Now, now, nothing to get worked up about. We've known for ages that all's not right about this place, but we've agreed to stay. No cause to change our minds now. If we keeps our noses out of it, nothin' will 'appen to us. Rea, do eat that thing!" .

Rea forced a mouthful or two down, glad that the others were quiet for a moment, busy with their tea. The light of the fire was on Millie's face, but it looked like a bloodstain, and she cringed again.

"No one said anythin' about that doll," she said finally. "Not even them policemen."

"Well, no they wouldn't, don't suppose." Mrs Butcher was rocking backwards and forwards, at her ease. Another fifteen minutes or so before she need get up to see to dinner. "Wouldn't mean nothin' to them, would it?"

Rea's voice was softer than ever.

"It went, you know. I looked out of the winder later, and it weren't there."

Mrs Butcher's lips compressed.

"No, don't 'spect it was. They'd 'ave moved it, wouldn't they? Them police, I mean."

"I think it was that what killed 'er."

They rounded on Rea, hushing her up with a single voice.

"Don't never say nothin' like that again." The treat was spoilt, and Millie was getting to her feet. "You ought to know better. Now come and 'elp me with the vegetables. Meat's in, and soup's comin' along nicely. Just the fish, sweet, and savoury to see to. Come on."

She hauled Rea to her feet, hustling her over to the sink.

Tottie May put her plate aside regretfully. Muffins were her favourites, but they didn't last long, and now there was another whole month to wait.

"Believe Rea, do you?"

"What I believe is that we'd better keep our mouths shut," returned Effie shortly. "Come on, let's set the table."

"All right." Tottie May was in no hurry; she never was when there was work to be done. "But I says she's got the truth of it. That old tartar wouldn't never kill 'erself unless someone made 'er do it."

Effie didn't answer. Instead she looked over at Mrs Butcher.

"Mrs B., 'oo do you think was the true love what Mrs Pritchard mentioned in that letter?"

Millie didn't look up from the Pain de Rhubarb she was preparing.

"Got me own ideas, of course, but less said the better."

"Someone we know, you think?"

"What I think and what I don't think ain't none of your business, Effie McGee. Now get yourself into that dining-room and lay the table. You too, Tottie May, and makes sure them glasses shine proper."

When they were gone, she said softly:

"Rea."

"Yes, Mrs Butcher?"

"Whatever 'appens, don't you say nothin', will you? Don't talk, and then you can't get 'urt."

Rea nodded, feeling dead inside. She wouldn't talk, but that wouldn't make any difference. When it came to her turn, they wouldn't care that she'd kept silent. When they were ready, they'd take her, and she knew it.

There was an especially soft bloom on Noreen Rutter's cheeks when Denys went to see her on the following night. Her eyes were brighter too, and she was more attentive than ever.

"Got some nice bloaters for you, ducks. 'Ave 'em now, or a bit later?"

"Not really hungry."

"Later then." She sat by his feet, close to the fire. "So she's dead, eh? Out of the way at last. Oh, Denys, I never guessed you'd ... well ... you know."

Pritchard felt the oddest recoil, wishing he could move away from Noreen's hand which was stroking his knee. He'd wanted to see Marcelle dead often enough in the past, yet now it was done he couldn't get the sight of her face out of his mind. He hadn't realised what hanging could do to a human body; it made him want to retch every time he thought about it.

"Nothin' to stop you finishin' the job now."

He said nothing, willing Noreen to stop talking.

"Is there, Denys?" She twisted round to him, smiling tenderly. "Get the rest done, and then we'll be married."

"Married!"

The sharpness of his tone wiped the smile away, and she was equally tart.

"Why yes, that's what you've always said. You promised ..."

"Not now!" His violence was subdued. "Not for a while, Nor, for God's sake! She not in her grave yet. Can't be for months, our gettin' hitched, I mean."

"Months?" Her voice rose higher. "I'm not waitin' too long, as I've told you plenty 'o times in the past. Two or three months, if you must, just for decency's sake, but then ..."

"Longer than that. Family wouldn't understand."

"They don't 'ave to, do they?" She relaxed, laughing as she settled back again. "Silly old Denys, they don't count any more. Once you've ..."

"I don't want to talk about it to-night."

"Well, we've got to talk about it soon. Make plans."

"Later on."

She turned round again, searching his face.

"Anyone 'ud think you cared about the old cow. You said you 'ated 'er. Didn't you? Was you lyin'?"

"No, I ha ... I didn't care for her much."

"Well, then ..."

"She's only just died, Nor. For pity's sake, let's leave it for now."

"Don't know that I can." She was fluffing up her hair, letting him see the rise and fall of her bosom under a thin blouse. "I likes to know where I am. Now, either you wants me or you don't. If you do, then you'll ..."

"Shut up! For Christ's sake, shut up! Shut up!"

She drew away from him, terrified by his expression, totally bewildered as she saw the ugly rage in him. She'd never seen him like this before; never. He looked half-mad, his eyes wild, his mouth working.

"Denys ..."

She waited as he struggled with the torment in him, all coquetry forgotten as she kept very still, expecting a blow across the face. Then it was over and he was back in his chair.

"You'll have to wait, Noreen," he said, and there was a new and unexpected firmness in him. "I can't have you pestering me like this. You'll get what you want, all in good time, but you'll have to be patient. D'yer hear me?"

"Yes, Denys."

She was very meek, kneeling at his feet. He'd frightened the life out of her for a minute back there, but now the fear was mixed with a tingling excitement. She'd never believed Denys had it in him. First, settling his wife's hash, and now threatening her with the hardness of his look. She'd always thought him a bit of a mouse, pleading for her favours, not demanding them. Not much spice in that. Now it was different.

"Do you want to ...?" She put one hand on the brooch at the neck of her blouse. "Shall we ...?"

"No, at least not for a while. Just be still and give me a minute's peace."

"Yes, Denys."

It was really rather thrilling to think that if she moved or disobeyed him he might thrash her within an inch of her life. That was the sort of lover she could really respect. After all, who wanted a tame husband when all was said and done?

It seemed to her that she had knelt there for ages before she realised that he was looking at her differently, and she even managed a blush, although after the life she'd led, it wasn't easy.

"We'll have that off," said Denys, his hand on her collar. "Can't stay here all night, you know."

She gasped as he ripped the blouse open, tearing the cheap chiffon as if it were a rag. He didn't fumble with the corset that night either; it was off in a second or two, and his hand was hard on her shoulder.

"Well, come on." He jerked her to her feet. "I've told you I've not got long."

"No, but even if you've got to go to-night, maybe soon you won't have to."

Their eyes locked and she blanched.

"Sorry, Denys, I didn't mean ..."

"So you should be." He was master at last, and it was a good feeling. No one to nag him narrow at home, and Nor no longer teasing and taunting him, granting him privileges as if her body were made of gold. "Get up to that bed, or I'll give you what for, and keep your mouth shut."

She almost ran up the steps, heart unsteady, not sure that fear was not getting the better of excitement, standing by the bed waiting for him. He looked at her for a long while, studying every inch of her until she began to squirm.

"Denys!"

"I told you to shut up."

He hit her across the face with the back of his hand, feeling six foot tall as she collapsed whimpering across the bed.

Loving Noreen that night was better than it had ever been before. She was no less anxious to be taken, and their relationship had assumed a new gloss. He gave the orders, she obeyed them.

It wasn't until he got back to Chantry Close, and had opened the front door, that the euphoria dissolved into fear and guilt again. He'd only taken a few steps when he heard it, as plain as anything.

"Denys, is that you? You're very late. Where have you been? Couldn't get a cab, I suppose?"

He was grey as he climbed the stairs. There hadn't been anything else; just those few words. He waited a long time before turning the handle and going into the room which he and Marcelle had shared. It was empty, as he knew it had to be. Marcelle was dead. She had been found hanging from a tree in the garden.

Yet it had been her voice which had called to him down there in the darkness. Impossible or not, he knew he was right. It had been Marcelle, and he hurried into the dressing-room and bolted the door behind him.

When Philippe caught hold of Regina's arm in a vice-like grip and half-dragged her into the parlour, she was taken completely unaware. The anger in him was obvious; as plain as the long fingers gripping her and bruising her so callously.

"You've been talking to Loveday Preece," he said finally, his voice as harsh as his hold. "Why did you tell her you didn't think Marcelle had killed herself? You little fool? Why are you forever making mischief?"

At last she managed to tug herself free, feeling her dignity ruffled, and very much aware that her heart was thumping unevenly.

"I shall say what I want to whom I please. Preece asked me if I thought Marcelle had committed suicide. I simply said no, I didn't think so."

"Why not?" He glared at her. "She admitted it, didn't she? She said she was going to take her own life. What more do you want?"

"Perhaps she didn't write the letter."

"Don't be absurd, of course she did. You know it was her handwriting."

"Perhaps someone made her do it."

He raised his hands in exasperation.

"How can you make a person do such a thing?"

"It's possible."

"I can't think how. In any event, you have no right to discuss such matters with the servants."

"I told you," she retorted hotly, "I wasn't discussing it with Loveday. I merely answered one question, that's all."

"And that was enough."

"I wish you'd ..."

He broke into her sentence with scant ceremony.

"Jeanne has brought her mother's diary to me."

Regina paused. Philippe was sombre, but no longer angry.

"Jeanne brought it to you? Why you?"

"Perhaps she trusts me, which is more than you do, isn't it?"

She could feel herself colouring up, but he was opening the

book, not worrying about her confusion.

"When one reads this, there's not much doubt that Marcelle had a lot on her conscience. The woman was a whore. She cuckolded Denys many times, and boasts of it."

"Does she say who the men were?"

"Well, Dummer, for one. There are a few other names mentioned, but they mean nothing to me. They wouldn't, of course, for I've only just arrived."

Regina didn't pick him up on that. There was another matter of more importance on her mind at that moment.

"And her true love? Who was he?"

It was as if a blind had gone down behind the grey eyes, lids dropping in their customary fashion to conceal whatever he was thinking.

"She doesn't say."

"Don't you think that is rather strange?"

"Not particularly. Perhaps she preferred to keep his name secret, even in her private diary."

"Which isn't very private now, is it?" She was terse. "I wonder what Marcelle would think if she knew you were reading it."

"I have no idea."

His voice was toneless, keeping all feeling out of it.

"I wouldn't have thought Marcelle could love anyone like that. She wasn't that sort of woman."

"Any sort of woman can love like that, once in a life-time."

"I'm sure you're most expert in such matters."

"Don't be childish, Regina."

"Too close to home?"

"I think this conversation has lasted long enough." He turned away. "Remember what I said. This is not a subject for gossiping to the servants about. Whatever Marcelle did, and however she decided to end her life, it is a family matter."

"I do not need you to teach me my manners, and it seems to me to be a perfectly reasonable thing to try to find out who this man was. He may have had something to do with her death."

"I wouldn't try, if I were you. Your life could be at risk."

"At your hands, Philippe?" She forced herself to be calm, although her fingers were tightly clenched where he couldn't see them. "Are you afraid of what I am going to ask next?"

That night, Regina sat in the drawing-room after everyone had gone to bed and considered the facts, and some other matters which weren't facts at all.

She was quite convinced now that Lavisse had not been Marcelle's lover. Her suspicion on that score was quashed at last. The cool, fastidious Philippe would never have wanted Marcelle, but if Marcelle had discovered the reason for his presence at Chantry Close, and if he had deemed it wise to silence her, he might well have persuaded her that he found her attractive, and arranged a rendezvous on the night of her death.

It was a real possibility. If Marcelle had guessed that Philippe wanted Marionette's money, but was aware that her wealth would not be his until she was dead, Lavisse looked the kind of man who would not have let a fat, middle-aged shrew stand in his way.

But there were other things, much harder to link to Philippe Lavisse than these. She didnt' want to think about them, because she was alone, but the thoughts came anyway. The puppet of Marcelle, appearing first on the bed, then on the stairs, and finally on the tree. The puppet which could no longer be found, once Marcelle's body had been cut down. The almost human replica of Conrad Von Heltz, brilliant blue eyes of glass staring at her in derision.

Marta Rosa, the midget prima donna, who had been missing. The voice which was silent, now that Marta was home again where she belonged.

When she was with others, it was easier to find logical explanations for the appearance of the dolls in the house; when she was by herself, she could find none. The sense of foreboding she had had on her arrival had increased a hundredfold, fed by Marionette's reputation, and that queer, inexplicable feeling she could create of drawing someone to her. And the dolls. Tired of the workshop, Rea had said; wanting the house for themselves.

She got up abruptly. She must stop it, or she really would go mad. A warm drink and then bed. In the kitchen she started to mix cocoa powder with milk, when she saw the glimmer outside.

She knew before she got to the window who it was she would see. Tall, dark hair just visible by the lantern, as on the previous occasion, making his way to the shed where a dim light burnt in the window.

He was going to Eda Trott, that was obvious. Not Marcelle, perhaps, but Eda certainly. Lovely, lovely Eda, who was brave enough to sleep in that place with the marionettes. Why wasn't Eda afraid of them?

Regina poured the milk down the sink, no longer wanting it. Eda wasn't afraid because she didn't live in the house. She wasn't in their way, and so she had no cause to dread them.

She went upstairs, wondering what she would see, but there was nothing. The stairs were clear, and her own bedroom was just as she had left it. She was so low, that even when she thought again about Marta Rosa, her nerves didn't twitch. All she could think about was Philippe, on his way to see Louis's sewing-woman.

If this was love, no wonder Marcelle killed herself because of it. She moved to the window, although she knew she wouldn't be able to see anything. As she pulled the curtains back, the sharp certainty returned like the cut of a knife.

Marcelle hadn't killed herself for love, or for any other reason. Someone else had done that, but who was there strong enough to heave the body up to the branch of a tree? If Marcelle had been dead already, her neck broken, there would have been no struggle, of course; simply a question of raising the corpse until its feet were just off the ground, and knocking over the box.

Who had hated Marcelle enough to find that kind of strength? Who was determined enough, bitter enough, or even mad enough, to achieve murder and disguise it as suicide?

Who had Marcelle offended to such a degree that she had signed her own death warrant? The curtains were crumpling in Regina's tight grip. Preece had said Marionette was jealous of

Marcelle because the latter had a new lover, and Preece was a very strong woman.

But it wasn't only Marcelle Pritchard's body which had been hanging there. The marionette had been there too. A puppet couldn't have aroused Marionette's fury, surely, unless it had been a kind of sick joke.

But if the puppet itself had offended, then it had offended its own kind, not a human being.

Regina jerked the curtains together so hard that the heavy wooden rings clattered complainingly.

Oh, dear God! What was going on in No: 7, Chantry Close?

Jeanne went into her mother's room the next morning. She didn't really know why; perhaps just to enjoy the sense of freedom which had been hers since Marcelle had died. She'd seen her father go out, and Tottie May had already swept and dusted, so she wouldn't be disturbed.

Her heart began to race as she saw the figure by the bureau, trying to get out of the door before she was seen, but it was too late.

"What are you doing here?" Victor was furious, rage distorting his mouth. "Snooping again, you brat?"

One hand was tight about her hair, making her eyes water: the other held the painting, a small package still attached to it. She moaned, pointing to it, trying to mouth words.

"What is it, dummy?" He was cruel, twisting her plait harder than ever. "You know what this is, I'll bet. I've seen you creeping in here when you thought no one was about. You knew she'd got this, didn't you?"

She was struggling to free herself, but Victor liked hurting people, and she knew he wouldn't let her go yet.

"Did you take any of the money?" He jeered. "What do you want with money, an ugly bitch like you? Thought you'd buy some clothes to make yourself look better, was that it? Wouldn't make any difference. You'd still be a sight."

She was making noises now which seemed to spur him on. He let her hair go and jerked her arm behind her.

"Listen," he breathed in her ear, eyes dangerously bright, "if you ever let anyone know you've seen me here, it'll be the end of you. People who upset me don't live long, you know."

He saw her terror and laughed.

"That makes you think, doesn't it? And another thing. If anyone finds out, I'll smash that doll which looks like you into a thousand pieces, and that'll be the end of you. You'll go the same way; broken into splinters."

Her moans grew louder.

"Don't like that, do you?" He pushed her away contemptuously. "Scared stiff of those bits of wood, aren't you? Well, you know what to do. Keep quiet."

She watched him take some banknotes, replacing the package and hanging the picture back in its place.

"I'll say you took them, if they're found missing." He tucked the money away in his pocket. "I'll say I saw you."

Outside, he met Rea coming up with a pail to wash the window sills on the upper floors. He looked at her suspiciously, wondering if she'd heard anything, but when she gave a hasty bob and scuttled past him, he went downstairs whistling.

After a while, Jeanne came out of Marcelle's room, her face like stone. In her own bedroom she put on her shabby coat, pulled a scarf round her neck, and went down the back stairs. She met no one as she opened the door, letting herself out into the garden. Even if she had seen anyone, they wouldn't have thought much about it. Just poor, ugly Jeanne, going for a walk.

The door of the shed was open, and she could see Mrs Trott, back turned, working on some blue silk. She slipped past the seamstress, so light on her feet that Eda didn't even turn her head. Behind the curtains Jeanne screwed up her courage, fingers unsteady as she searched hastily amongst the dolls until she found what she was looking for.

She knew they were all watching her, seeing what she was doing, but she didn't care. It was a matter of self-preservation, nothing more, and she tip-toed out as quietly as she had gone in.

In her room she laid the thing on her bed, contemplating it with a sinking heart. In her hurry, she'd got the wrong one. It stared up at her, its painted smile scornful at her incompetence. Quickly she thrust it into a drawer, rushing out of the room again as if the Devil were after her, oblivious to everything but her desire to get away.

After she had gone, there was a movement in the shadows on the landing; a figure waiting until the sound of Jeanne's steps could be heard in the hall before it came forward.

After luncheon, Jeanne could bear it no longer. She'd have to put it back, or get rid of it some other way. It couldn't be allowed to stay in her room all night. She opened the drawer, stopping abruptly, one hand frozen in mid-air. Then the frantic search amongst shabby underwear and darned black stockings, but it was no good. It wasn't there.

She knelt on the floor, shivering. No one could have seen her take it. Certainly no one could have looked through a closed door and seen her hide it, yet it had vanished just the same.

The answer was simple, of course, and Jeanne rested her head against the chest, the strength draining out of her.

No one had taken it. It had gone by itself.

Nine

"I don't think these things which have been happening here are accidents at all."

Regina said it defiantly, and waited for Lavisse to contradict her. They had met on their way down to breakfast: Regina pale from lack of sleep, Philippe's demeanour as usual. She almost hated him for his detachment, and had come to the point where she had to know whether he was involved or not. Awake, she thought of him constantly; asleep she dreamt of him, but what sort of man was he?

"Really?"

"Yes, really." She was not put off by his apparent indifference to her emphatic statement. If he had hoped to keep her quiet by pretending to ignore her words, he would be unlucky. "And what is more, I think I know who is responsible."

They had almost reached the breakfast-room, pausing just long enough for Lavisse to study the frightened eyes looking up into his, and for Regina's heart to flutter anxiously when she saw the line of his mouth.

Of course she didn't know. She wasn't even sure that what had gone on were deliberate acts or not. At least, not deliberate acts taken by those who lived at No: 7. The flutter became a thump. She mustn't think of them now. She had to know whether Philippe was involved.

"Then you have dangerous knowledge." The smile barely moved his lips, the lids shielding his thoughts as always. "You will have to be careful, won't you?"

She sat at table more uncertain than ever. Had Lavisse been

threatening her, or had he known she was bluffing? She accepted coffee, refusing food. Effie clicked her tongue in disapproval.

"Should eat, Miss Regina, 'specially on a cold mornin' like this. Nice bit o' haddock? Or some sausages and bacon?"

She managed to control the queasiness which beset her, and shook her head.

"Nothing, thank you, Effie."

Louis wasn't eating either, but after the meal was done, he said in a conspiratorial whisper:

"I've done it, Regina! I've done it!"

She almost cried out, pulling herself together when she saw his beam. She was behaving absurdly, imagining everyone's thoughts were like her own.

"What, Uncle Louis?"

He chuckled.

"My life-sized marionette. It's finished. Will you come and see it this evening? Unfortunately, I've got to go out now, and I doubt that I'll be back until after dinner."

"To-night?"

The thought of another visit to the workshop after dark appalled her. He saw it, and his face fell, as if she had just snatched something very precious from him.

"You don't want to see it."

His voice was flat, the eagerness gone, as if someone had wiped his face clean like a slate. She couldn't let it happen. So many people had disappointed Louis Boussard, and made him feel unwanted. She couldn't do that too.

"Of course I want to see it; you know that. It was just that I thought to-night ... well ..."

The hope was back, his voice lifting.

"You're worried about the workshop after dark? No need. I'll be there, and so will Mrs Trott. She's staying on after she's finished her work, and she's as excited as I am about what we've done. Do say you'll come."

Regina found herself agreeing, despite the warning voice inside her, and Louis was all contentment again.

"Nine o'clock, then. I'm so looking forward to shewing you.

You're one of the few who have ever cared about my work, and I'll never forget that."

She went into the study and pretended to read a book. Louis had said she could go there any time she wished, and there wasn't anything else to do. She couldn't talk to Jeanne; she didn't want to talk to Denys or Victor. She certainly didn't want to go near Lavisse for a while.

She opened the last work by Mr Dickens, but the print danced up and down. All she could think about was her promise to Louis; a promise to go to the shed at nine o'clock that night. It was like a dead weight on her soul, until she forced herself to be rational. There was nothing to be afraid of. Louis would be there, and so would Mrs Trott.

She made herself pay attention to the novel, refusing to heed the whisper in her mind which reminded her that Eda and Louis would not be the only ones present. They would be there too.

Dinner finished earlier than usual. By eight-thirty it was over, and Effie was coming in to clear. Regina felt light-headed, for she hadn't touched the ox-tail soup, the sole, or the roast sirloin of beef, even ignoring Millie's delicious Gâteau de Riz and ice pudding. No breakfast, no lunch, no dinner: little wonder that she felt faint. She scolded herself as she went up to say goodnight to Marionette before keeping her tryst with Louis and his new treasure.

On the landing she heard shouting, waiting nervously. Abruptly, the door was thrown open and Victor rushed out. He saw her, and yet he didn't. His face was screwed up with rage, his voice rough as he said bitterly:

"I'll kill her! Hateful old toad, I'll finish her off one day, see if I don't."

Regina had hardly recovered from Victor's spleen, when she encountered Marionette's own fury.

"Deceitful oaf!" Marionette's mouth was like a trap. "I'll see he pays for what he's done. I may not always have seen eye to eye with Marcelle, but I won't let him escape justice for what he did to her."

Regina's legs almost gave way, but she got to the stool in time.

"What he did to her, Aunt Marionette?"

The anger died instantly: snuffed out.

"Never mind. It's none of your affair, but he'll pay the price, don't you worry."

"You mean that you think he ..."

Regina couldn't say it aloud; the words wouldn't come. What had Victor done to his mother? His mother, who had been found strung up on a tree?

"You look terrible." Marionette was brutally honest. "What's the matter with you, girl? Aren't you well?"

"Yes, of course." Regina wished she'd taken a moment to touch her cheeks with rouge, but that wouldn't have disguised the smudges under her eyes. "I'm quite all right."

"Liar." Marionette was taking in every hair of Regina's head, searching her face, noting the hands clasped tightly together against sea-green velvet. "Still, it's your business, I suppose. Better get an early night. You look as though you need it."

"I think I will." Regina rose in relief. The scrutiny was too thorough to bear any longer, and she did not want Marionette to know that she was going to the workshop. Marionette didn't approve of Louis's hobby. "Good-night."

"Good-night, sleep well."

Marionette waited until Regina had opened the door before she added very softly:

"If you can, my dear, if you can."

Regina slipped out of the house without encountering anyone. She saw the long-case clock in the hall with its hands standing at five minutes to nine, closing the door quietly behind her and using her lantern to guide her through the garden.

The bitter wind cut into her, and once she nearly turned back. Just in time she remembered Louis's pleading expression, and willed herself to go on. There was nothing to worry about. Louis would be there, with Eda Trott. Even if Eda was in love with Philippe, she was at least a human being, and she wasn't afraid of them. She lived and worked with them: they had no effect on her.

The door was open, but when Regina went in there was no sign of Eda or Louis either. The place where Louis carved wood and moulded wax was cleared for the night; tools put away, a sheet covering the brocades and velvets. Whatever Eda was doing, she wasn't working.

Regina moved on. The auditorium was deserted too, just enough colza lamps here and there to shew that she was alone. She called out, her voice unsteady, but there was no reply. She almost retreated again, but the thought of Louis's childlike excitement stopped her. She couldn't go yet. She had to meet him as she had promised, and doubtless he was behind the curtains, so deeply engrossed in what he was doing that he hadn't heard her.

She went up the steps very slowly, keeping her eyes shut when she reached the place where Louis had to lean over the bridge to work the controls: the place where they hung on their hooks, waiting for him to take them down and give them life.

Finally, she had to look, feeling the last of her courage seeping away. There were so many of them, and they were all watching her. Their glittering eyes seemed to move as she moved, following her progress. She had forgotten that Eda and Louis should have been there, too mesmerized by the sight of their handiwork. Some, in pretty gowns, with pink wax cheeks and silky curls made of human hair were beautiful, but they were horrible too. Others made no pretence of loveliness; drab and plain, but equally heart-stopping.

Her mind was commanding her to remember that they were only marionettes, but her heart was denying it. The clown was grinning at her, and she could have sworn that one of the ballerinas moved an arm.

She thought she heard a noise, and mouthed Louis's name again, no sound coming from her paralysed lips as she became aware at last of what she had come to see.

It hung a few feet away from her, on a peg like the rest of

them, but it was the size of a human being, as Louis had said it would be. It wore a white gown, which was very familiar, and when she got nearer, she realised it was her own dress; the one which Marionette had admired not long ago. She let her gaze move upwards. The hair was silver-fair, dressed as hers was, the head drooping. Closer still, the lantern raised an inch or two more. The eyes were very blue, like hers; the mouth deep rose, like hers; the cheekbones high, like hers; the nose small and narrow; like hers.

She moaned under her breath. She was looking at herself. Every feature was the same, even down to the beauty spot on the left side of her face. She couldn't stay another second, and yet she couldn't move either. It was a nightmare, but one from which there was no awakening. She just stood there, bewitched by her double, until she saw a candle coming towards her.

The nape of her neck was prickling as the outline of a man became clearer, head half-hidden in shadows. He was tall and dark, she knew that, and when he spoke it was in a whisper.

"Do you like it? Clever, isn't it? Old Louis did a good job, don't you think? You look like twins, not a jot of difference between you."

She tried to raise her lantern, but the whisper became a command.

"No! Don't do that. Keep still." The brief anger was gone, the soft huskiness amused again. "Feel it; touch it. You'll be surprised how real he's made it."

Regina didn't want to, but she knew she had to. The man would make her, no matter how terrified she was as she stretched out towards what was beside her. It was soft and yielding, but not like a stuffed object. It was as if it were a real person; a body made of flesh and blood. She moaned again, her hand falling to her side.

"Don't be afraid." The man was soothing. "After all, it's you, isn't it? You're not afraid of yourself, are you?"

Regina tried to step backwards, but there was a small trunk on the stage which she hadn't seen. As she stumbled, she clutched at the hanging figure in an involuntary effort to save herself. It spun round slowly on its hook, the force of her grasp shifting the mask. She steadied herself, mouth opening in disbelief as the face began to slip. An inch or two at first, then more, and more, and finally down to the neck, so that what was underneath the painted wax was revealed with shattering clarity by the man's candle.

"Oh my God!" She shrieked at him. "What have you done? Oh, no! What have you done?"

"Not me." He was unmoved. "Louis did that."

She could feel herself growing colder and colder, her mind beginning to reel. She knew that if she remained where she was, she would die, and regardless of the man's order, she raised her light so that she could see him, hardly hearing his muffled curse.

"Oh no!"

First, she had thought nothing could be worse than the watchful puppets. Then she had believed no fear could be deeper than the sight of her double. After that, when she had seen the real face, she was convinced that there was no greater shade of dread she could experience, but again she had been wrong.

She saw the black, slightly curled hair first; then the powdered skin of the forehead and chin. The cheeks were heavily rouged, the mouth thickly coated with crimson. It was an obscenity, which stood straight and erect, holding itself proudly.

"I ... know you," she said finally, the words only a thread of sound. "I know you ... and yet I don't. You remind me of ... but you can't be he ... you can't be ..."

When he took a pace towards her, she found enough strength to shout at him.

"No! Keep away, keep away! Don't come near me, whoever you are. Go away! For pity's sake, don't touch me!"

She knew he wasn't going to listen to her, and her voice died in her throat. All she could do was to stand there and wait for him to do what he had come for. Another step and then another.

When he stopped, stiffening as if in agony, she found herself clutching at the body by her side, unconscious now of what it was. She was wholly transfixed by the distorted face, and the blood which welled up at the corner of the man's mouth, as if his lip-salve had melted, and was running down his chin.

As he pitched forward, Regina looked across his body at the final horror, her hold on the white dress tightening.

It was beyond belief, yet it was true. She was there, with a sharp chisel in her hand, stained red. Regina breathed a single word before her hysteria began.

"Marionette!"

She could hear herself screaming, the piercing noise splitting her skull, but she couldn't stop. For a second she took her eyes off the woman in front of her to look down at what lay at her own feet. The man gave one last convulsive twitch, and it was over.

Regina had fainted.

Nearly an hour later, everyone was in the sitting-room, even Marionette, lying on a settee by the fire. The servants huddled together at the door, keeping a wary eye on the two uniformed policemen and a thick-set man holding a hard hat between his stubby fingers. Rea, near to collapse, had been allowed an upright chair, but only Effie's steadying hand prevented her from tipping off it on to the floor.

Regina was not ashamed that she was trembling. It had been the most ghastly night of her life, and one she knew she would never forget. She stole a look at Philippe, leaning negligently against the mantelpiece. Thank God it hadn't been him. Oh, thank God! He gave her a smile which thawed some of her inner chill, producing a mite of comfort.

Jeanne was like one dead, whilst her brother's bombast had all gone. He was a pricked balloon, huddling in a chair next to his father's, as if he were trying to hide himself away.

Regina said slowly:

"I don't understand." Her throat hurt, because of the frantic screams which had poured from it when she had looked over the prone body and seen Marionette, but the ache was nothing. That would pass. "Who was it? I thought for a moment that it was …"

"Philippe?" Marionette gave a short laugh. "I can assure you it wasn't."

"Then who? I don't understand." Regina seemed to be saying the same thing over and over again, but she was still numb, her mind clogged. "Who was it ... that ... thing I saw ... that terrible, painted creature?"

The man with the hat gave a discreet cough.

"I think we'd all like to know what's been going on Miss. You'll remember me, of course. I came here before, when that German gentleman died. Inspector Brewster from the local station. Mr Lavisse sent for me when Mrs Preece told him her mistress had gone from her room, and that there was a light in the workshop. He guessed something was seriously wrong, and so it was. Good thing he got to the shed in time." He was brisk and unemotional. To him, it was just another job; nothing painful to tear him apart. "Now, madame, suppose you ..."

"Marionette." Regina didn't mean to interrupt the inspector, but she couldn't help it. "You walked! I saw you. You walked!"

The inspector's small, intelligent eyes went from one woman to the other, but he kept silent, waiting to see what Mme. Boussard would say.

"It was you ... you who stabbed him, wasn't it?" Regina was shaking again. "You had a chisel in your hand and it was all red. You killed that man ... but ... but who was he? Was it really ...?"

"Better get it over." Brewster was calm, not hurrying Marionette, but encouraging her as if she were a child. "It's got to be said, you know, so why not now?"

Marionette flicked a disinterested glance in his direction.

"Why not, indeed? It's finished anyway, but you won't like it. You may not even believe it, but it's true."

"Let's judge for ourselves, shall we?" Brewster had a notebook in his hand. "Start at the beginning, will you, so there's no misunderstanding?"

Marionette gave him a last contemptuous look, but she didn't argue, and reduced to its barest bones, her gruesome story was almost as incredible as she had said it would be. It was also totally frank, as if she were stripping her innermost self, piece by piece, for everyone to see.

It seemed that when she had first met Louis Boussard, he had been in the theatre. Originally a stage hand; then promoted to making costumes and masks; finally, because of his quite extraordinary good looks, to the boards themselves. But even his beauty couldn't make a Thespian of him, and when he had encountered Mademoiselle Marigny, and had seen her instant attraction to him, he was quite glad to quit the stage and settle for the life of a gentleman. He had no particularly strong feelings for Marionette, but she was young, comely, and a rich man's daughter.

They'd been content enough at first. She, genuinely and passionately in love with him; he, just good enough an actor to make her believe he returned the same degree of devotion. Soon, however, it came to Marionette's ears that Louis was seeing another woman, and she paused in her narrative to confess that her rage had been like a roaring furnace, consuming her to ashes, although she had never let him see it. In spite of her riches, jealousy might drive him off, and, to her, an adulterous Louis was better than no Louis at all.

In a way, the coach accident had been a God-send, for it gave her a chance to salvage her tattered pride, and keep Louis into the bargain. Vernon Morse, a disreputable, unethical physician, with a penchant for gambling at which he was consistently unlucky, was happy enough to accept a generous annual retainer to confirm that Marionette was both maimed and bedridden. It was a secret shared by Morse, Marionette, and Loveday Preece only, and then Marionette had been able to hold up her head again. She replaced all the servants, save Loveday, and started her new life, quite prepared to face the fact that it was going to be as constricting as any prison sentence. She didn't care. It wasn't that Louis didn't want to make love to her; he couldn't. She was crippled. When he found other women, she told herself that he was a red-blooded man, and since she couldn't give him what he wanted, he was bound to look elsewhere. She became almost proud of his virility. She had begun to believe her own lies.

She paused for a moment, glancing up.

"Vernon Morse thought Marcelle might have started to suspect

I was not as helpless as I seemed. He said we should do something about her, but, in the end, we didn't have to."

She went back to the tale, her gaze fixed on the sparkling rings again.

Ten years later, she had discovered that Louis was engaged in a liaison with one of their parlourmaids. Before the girl could be removed discreetly, Marionette had noticed a smear of fresh blood on Louis's cuff when he went to say good-night to her. The next morning, the servant was found with her wrists slashed, and four months pregnant. The world believed the story of suicide; Marionette did not.

When she taxed her husband, he had flown into a frenzy and opened her cheek with a pair of scissors, but even that she had forgiven him, particularly when he had knelt by her bed, his tears falling on her hand as he begged her to help him.

She knew other things would happen, for she had seen by then just how unstable he was. Yet he had to be protected, because her feeling for him was as fierce as ever it had been, and so she created the illusion that she had abnormal powers, and could do strange things which others couldn't do. Any odd occurrences would be laid at her door, and not at Louis's, yet she was safe enough. If, for any reason, the authorities were called in they could in no way blame her. How could she do anything? She was bedridden.

It wasn't difficult to produce the necessary aura of evil. It helped that Loveday, a simple country woman, still clung to folk-lore and the old religion, genuinely believing her mistress to be a witch, or wise woman. The tales she told of Marionette's power, and the servants' gossip, did the rest.

Louis, as cunning as he was unbalanced, had seen at once what his wife was doing, and had thrown himself whole-heartedly into helping her. No word on the subject was ever exchanged between them, but Marionette said it was he who hid in the empty closet next to her room, mimicking and throwing his voice, as he had done on the night of the puppet show, to make it appear that she was having terrible quarrels with the family and others living in the house. It hadn't been difficult. There was a knot-hole in the cupboard, just like the one in the press next to Jeanne's room.

A year after the maid's death, Louis fell dangerously ill. He recovered eventually but his superlative looks were gone. His hair and beard had turned grey; his skin was wrinkled; his eyes had lost their colour; his mind had toppled right over the brink of sanity. It was then that he began to create his own illusion, that of a frail and bent old man: kindly, gentle, harmless. But he wasn't too old to want women, his vanity was greater than ever, and he was far from harmless.

Marionette had kept herself mobile by walking about her room at night, often venturing out into the passages very late, when she thought everyone else had retired. Once, she had seen someone coming up the stairs, flattening herself against the wall as the person drew closer to her, his face lit from below by the candle in his hand. She admitted, in a voice momentarily shaky, that she had nearly collapsed, for she had hardly recognised him.

He wore a dark wig, beard and moustache, with pads in his cheeks to fatten them. He also stood straight, made taller by the height of the heels of his shoes, but it was Louis right enough. Boussard might not have been a very good actor, but he had learned how to use theatrical make-up, and he was trying to recapture the looks which had made him an idol to many.

When Loveday had told her mistress that someone was having *affaires* with Marcelle and Eda Trott, Marionette had understood. It was Louis, but they hadn't recognised him. They would always have met him in near-darkness, and they hadn't realised who their paramour was. He never made love to them in the house, but in the shed. One night, Marionette had seen Louis opening the side door to Eda, taking her hand in his.

"When Floss Baker fell down those stairs, I wondered if it was really an accident." Marionette looked unexpectedly grey. "I guessed that Louis was interested in the girl; she was a pretty thing. I was never quite certain, of course, but I think he killed her."

The garbled noises which suddenly spilled from Jeanne's

bloodless lips made everyone start as they turned to her, seeing her agonized distress as she pointed to her eyes.

Philippe said gently:

"Don't be frightened, Jeanne. You are telling us that you saw something?"

She nodded vigorously.

"What did you see? Try, it's important. Do you want to write it down?"

Jeanne's hands jerked abruptly outwards, as if she were thrusting someone away from her, and Marionette gave a shuddering sigh.

"She saw him do it. That's what she's trying to tell you. She saw Louis push the girl."

"But why didn't you get help ... write it down ... explain to your mother or to your father?" Regina was bewildered. "Why did you keep it to yourself for so long?"

"I can tell you why." Marionette's lids were closed. "She thought he might have seen her. That's it, isn't it?" The snapping black eyes were open again, fixed on Jeanne. "You thought Louis might have caught a glimpse of you, and you were convinced that he'd kill you too if you betrayed him."

Jeanne nodded once more, and Marionette said tiredly:

"The servants said it was I who had cursed Jeanne with dumbness, but I knew, of course, that it wasn't me. I thought it simply the result of the fever, but now I know better. It was shock. Louis didn't see you. If he had done, you wouldn't be here to-day."

Philippe was turning the pages of a book in his hand.

"This journal was where you said it would be, Marionette; in Louis's desk, hidden away. It's a complete record of everything he did, even the smallest detail. Why he should keep such incriminating evidence, I can't think."

"That's because you didn't know Louis." Marionette sounded far away. "He was a most meticulous man; always made notes of everything. When he ... well ... when he began to kill, he couldn't break the habit. Besides, he was very conceited. It would never have occurred to him that he'd be caught."

"I see." Philippe was looking at the next leaf. After a moment he glanced up at Jeanne with compassion. "There's more, isn't there? There's a secret which has been torturing you for weeks. Boussard says here that he came to your room several times and made love to you. I take it that's true?"

Jeanne made a quick motion with her hand, and the inspector gave her his notebook.

"Here, Miss, write it there."

When at last Jeanne had finished, Philippe quickly read through the scrawl, nauseated by the words.

"Yes, it's true, but she didn't know it was Louis. It was pitch black in her room, and she thought it was one of the puppets which had been given power to become the size of a man. She was sure Marionette had sent it to punish her for some reason. Moreover, she feared it was the doll which looked like her brother." He hesitated, seeing Jeanne's sick shame, passing over the next paragraph. The girl was suffering enough, without the others knowing how she had reacted to Boussard. "She dared not try to communicate what was happening to her. She was too afraid of the thing which she believed to be a demon. Finally, she took what she thought was Victor's likeness from the workshop. She was going to destroy it, she says, but then she found she'd taken the wrong one. It seems it disappeared from her room."

"Oh, Jeanne, dearest Jeanne." Regina concentrated on what Philippe had been reading, refusing to listen to an inner voice which had seized upon the last few words. "If you only had come to me, as I asked you to."

"She couldn't." Lavisse was bleak. "I've just told you; she was half out of her mind."

Regina didn't mind his anger; she understood it. He was thinking of Jeanne, and what she had been through. She said hesitantly:

"Does Louis say anything about the singing I heard? The woman's voice?"

"No, but undoubtedly it was he."

Regina felt her heart sink. Louis had been very meticulous, so Marionette had said, never missing a single detail. Surely he would have recorded that. Philippe saw her face, and swore to himself.

"Of course it was he, Regina. He could imitate anyone, you know that."

"And throw his voice." Marionette was watching her too. "I told you he was a ventriloquist, but you must have realised that when you saw the puppet show. He always made the dolls appear to talk."

"That settles it."

Philippe was done with the subject, but Regina wasn't. She couldn't forget Marta Rosa.

"What about the rest of the deaths?" Brewster took his pocket book back, mopping his brow discreetly. He hoped he would never get a case like this again. What had happened was right down evil. "That German, for instance."

Marionette turned to regard him caustically.

"Why, Inspector, you look quite wan. Too strong for your stomach, is it? Loveday get him a brandy." She went back to the contemplation of her rings. "You were asking about Von Heltz. I can tell you a bit. No doubt Louis's record will tell you the rest, for I'm sure he wouldn't have skipped over such an incident as that."

The grin was more fearsome than ever.

"Loveday saw Conrad coming out of the shed. He looked as if Satan was at his heels, and so she went into the workshop to see what was going on. All she could find was a mask on the floor which she brought to me."

The voice grated on her listeners' ears.

"Louis knew how to make them, as you know, but this wasn't any ordinary one. It was a death-mask of Dora Jones, that crippled woman who'd been my companion, and who'd disappeared. I'd seen enough of them in my time to recognise that, and I'd never believed those two women just went out early one morning and never came back, as Louis said they had done.

He swore they'd run off on their own accord, but remember, no one else saw them go but Louis." She paused. "Of course, in fact, they didn't go at all."

After a second she went on again.

"I told Loveday to put the mask back."

"And she did." Philippe was scanning the cramped handwriting. "But she put it back in the wrong place, and Louis noticed it. He also found the German's cigar case which he must have dropped as he ran. Boussard couldn't be sure whether Conrad realised the significance of what he'd seen. Perhaps he had, since he was so afraid. Anyway, Boussard writes that he returned the case to Conrad's room before the man knew he'd lost it, drugged his night drink, and later crept down and set fire to the room."

"Christ!" Brewster went scarlet, apologising at once for his language. "Sorry, ladies, but I just can't believe it. He seemed that upset when the German gentleman was found."

"Oh yes." Marionette was mildly amused. "Louis's talents as an actor increased with age. I've no doubt his performance was a good one."

"And the two companions?" Regina asked it fearfully. "What did happen to them?"

Philippe looked almost ill.

"They had rejected Boussard's overtures, and that was unforgivable. As Marionette says: he was a very conceited man. He killed them, and buried their bodies in the garden. It seems Miss Jones was an attractive woman, despite her disability, and Louis wanted her."

"Was Dummer's death accidental?"

"No." Lavisse's lips thinned. "Louis found out that Marcelle had slept with Dummer one night when he, Louis, had told her he was too busy to bother with her. Although he was tiring of her, he couldn't forgive her for the insult, nor Dummer either. Madness lent him strength to strike a blow on the back of Dummer's head, and to lever the stones down on top of the body." He grimaced. "At least, I assume it was madness which made him strong. Louis simply says it was an exhilarating experience."

Regina was near to tears.

"And Marcelle?"

"Yes, he killed her too. Not only because she'd made a fool of him, but because he thought she had started to suspect his identity. He didn't like the questions she was asking, it seems, and so he broke her neck and then put her on that tree with the puppet, hoping that everyone would think Marionette had done it."

"As, of course, they did." Marionette was sour. "It was always my fault."

"But your idea." Lavisse was short. "You elected to pose as a witch, so don't complain now at your success."

He went back to the diary.

"By now, he was becoming interested in someone else, but first, a few points of mystery are cleared up here." His long forefinger ran down a page. "These are some of the things people thought Marionette responsible for. It seems Louis was always turning off gasoliers and lamps; hiding behind doors and then pulling them slowly shut when he heard someone coming. He also put the glass eye in his wife's room that night; he imitated Marcelle's voice after she was dead and writes that Denys nearly died too; of fright."

Philippe's eyes grew hard.

"He says 'my beautiful niece was really afraid when my children came into the house.' It also seems that Boussard had an encounter in the attic with you, dear coz." He turned his head. "You asked why Jeanne didn't try to tell someone what was happening to her. You were no better. You mentioned this incident to no one, did you?"

Regina shook her head, giving her nose a small, defiant blow.

"Of course not. How could I?"

Philippe said something under his breath before going on.

"He put a footstool on the annexe stairs, and then made just enough noise outside my door to wake me up. By the time the rest of you got there, the stool was gone. He regretted that I wasn't killed at once, but he was planning to try again."

"But why? What had you done to him?"

"Nothing, but René's son was to inherit a good part of Marionette's fortune. Louis didn't like that."

"I see." Regina was biting her lower lip. "You said he was interested in someone else. Was that me?"

"Indeed it was." Marionette was venomous. "Never could resist a real beauty, and you're that all right. I could see all the signs. I knew he'd try to make love to you, and that the chances were that he'd make an end of you when you refused him, but this time I couldn't let him do it."

"Yes, I had wondered about that." Philippe eyed her curiously. "You have stood by for so long and let your lunatic husband terrify and kill. Why, now, has your conscience been roused? What was so special about Regina?"

Marionette didn't answer at first, but finally she said:

"She reminded me of myself when I was young. Not in looks, of course, but in other ways. You and she are in love, although maybe you've not admitted it to one another yet, just as Louis and I were once. When I saw the way things were going, I knew I couldn't let him do it. It would have been as if he were killing me."

Regina was very pink, but Lavisse took Marionette's comments in his stride.

"He was afraid that Rea might have seen him in the shed with Eda Trott one night. He tells how he drugged the girl, dressed her up in one of Regina's gowns, and put on the wig and mask he'd previously made. Later, he was going to finish the job. He'd heard what Regina said to me before breakfast, and really believed she knew the truth. Therefore, she had to die as well. He was going to kill two birds with one stone, but not until he'd … he'd … raped Regina."

The word was ugly in the air, and Marionette's face was the colour of clay.

Philippe glanced at the kitchenmaid, hunched up like a small bundle.

"Are you all right now, Rea?"

"Yes, sir."

"Is she, Mrs Butcher?"

"She'll do." Millie's lips were stiff, but she kept her shoulders back. First thing in the morning she'd be off to her sister's, taking Rea with her. Effie and Tottie May would have to fend for themselves. She'd had enough of this house and its horrors, and no wonder the child had looked so deathly. "Yes, sir, she'll be as right as rain with me."

"I couldn't believe it when I saw it." Regina was living the moment over again. "Its face was so like mine. I was looking at myself."

"I know, I saw the mask too." Lavisse touched her briefly on the shoulder. "Then, it appears, that Louis put on his disguise, only his hand must have been unsteady to-night." For once Philippe's iron control was shaken. "He'd made himself look like a nightmare. Heavy rouge, painted lips ... a gargoyle."

"I nearly died of fright." Regina was tearing at her lace-edged handkerchief. "In the darkness, I thought at first that it was you. No one else was so tall, or had dark hair."

Philippe's strong hand was over hers, stopping the tremors.

"There was blood on his mouth as he fell towards me. Oh, it was dreadful! He almost touched me ... and ... and then I saw Marionette."

"Yes, I know, that's when I arrived." Philippe shot Marionette a look of pure hatred. "Your change of heart came somewhat late, madame."

She shrugged, uncaring again.

"Maybe, but I've told you all you need to know. The journal will fill in the rest. Now, before these gentlemen take me away, as I'm sure they intend to do, let me ask a few questions of my own. You, my girl, who are you? Your French is perfect, and you know a great deal about my family, but you're not Regina Curtis. Whoever coached you, overlooked one small, but important, thing. Obviously they hadn't been told about it. You see, Regina Curtis died three months ago. Louis and the others didn't know that either; that's why they accepted you."

Regina could feel Philippe's eyes on her, but she avoided looking at him, answering Marionette as if he wasn't there.

"Oddly enough, my name is Regina, but not Curtis, as you say. I'm Regina Kendall, and Dora Jones was my mother's nurse-companion. I came here because I had a debt to pay. Three years ago, we were on holiday in the country. I was riding, when suddenly my horse started to bolt. Dora was ahead of me, and when she saw what was happening, she flung herself at the reins. She managed to stop the animal, but her hip was broken, and it never really mended. I used to watch her walk about, running pointless errands for my mother, and I could tell that she was in pain. Pain, which was my fault. When my mother died, I begged Dora to stay with me, but she wouldn't. She thought I was offering her charity because of what she'd done. She said I had too many friends to need a companion, and I was as healthy as an ox and wouldn't know what to do with a nurse. Besides, she wanted to go on helping the sick: she liked that kind of work. After she came to Chantry Close, she wrote a few times, yet her letters didn't feel right. Later, we arranged that she should come and see me, but she never arrived, nor did I get a note explaining why. That was totally out of character for Dora. She always kept her word. She said she would come, but she didn't.

"I wasn't sure what to do at first, but then her brother, Percival Jones, called to see me. He was worried too, for his letters addressed to her here had been returned, marked 'gone away', and she hadn't let him know where she was. Percival is a gentleman's gentleman, as he put it, and he said his master had been very kind and understanding. He'd suggested that Percival should go to the police. He did, but when the police made enquiries, and were told that Dora had gone of her own free will, there was nothing they could do.

"That was when I decided to find out more about Mme. Boussard and her family. I had lived in France most of my life, and I soon learned about Yvette Curtis and her daughter. Language was no problem, and friends and acquaintances told me enough of Mme. Boussard and her relations to enable me to pose as her niece. The one thing they didn't know, of course, was that Regina was dead."

At last Regina looked up at Philippe.

"I didn't like the deception, but I was so sure that something had happened to Dora. I sensed it very strongly and I couldn't just ignore it. I had to know the truth. Dora saved my life; I was trying to save hers."

"A most excellent act, Miss Kendall." Marionette sounded as though she meant it. "Almost as good as Louis's. And you, M. Philippe? Who are you? No blood relation of mine, that I know. I was aware from the start that the pair of you were not who you claimed to be, but I wasn't sure whether you meant Louis some harm, or were after my money, and so I said nothing and waited for you to make your move. Loveday kept an eye on you both. There wasn't much you did that I wasn't told about."

"I can believe it." Philippe glanced at Loveday, stolid as ever, with no expression on her whey-coloured face. "As you kept a watch on Mr Pritchard?"

Marionette's lip curled.

"That feeble, lazy, good-for-nothing? I've known for years that he wouldn't recognise Haydn from Bach. I had Dummer follow him not so long ago. He's got a doxy now somewhere in Lambeth, whom he visits. I could accept that, but the other night he tried to steal my jewels; my precious, precious jewels."

She looked like a snake, coiled to strike and Regina quivered.

"I thought at first it was Victor, but it was you, Denys, wasn't it? Victor just stole money from his mother. He denied it when I accused him, but Loveday saw him in Marcelle's room, after she was dead, taking more. Hateful little ghoul."

Pritchard was completely broken. Marionette's story, which had shaken him almost to insensibility, made the truth burst out of him, his admission leaving nothing unsaid.

"I meant you no harm," he concluded, the tears wet on his cheeks. "Noreen and I never intended to hurt you. We hoped Marcelle would be going away for a day or two soon; she had spoken of visiting friends. Then I was going to try to get the jewellery, so Nor and I could be together. That's all we wanted."

"And now all you'll get is prison," returned Marionette coldly, "and serve you right. But what of you, M. Lavisse, or whatever your name is? Who are you?"

"I'm Percival Jones's kind and understanding employer." He gave Regina another wry smile. "A small world, isn't it? My name is Vere Falkendon, and when the police could do nothing, and I saw how desperately worried Percival was, I decided to help him. I'm rich, idle, and was rather bored, and it seemed at the time to be a reasonable way of passing the time. My parents keep an *appartement* in Paris, and I've spent a good deal of time there. Like Regina, I've many friends in France, and it wasn't hard to get information about the Boussards and the Curtis family. I soon learned about René and his son." The smile was gone, the lines at the side of his mouth deeply etched. "If I had but known what I was taking on! When I found a blood-stained frock in the empty attic, I took it to London to shew Percival. He confirmed it was his sister's. Dear God, how I wish I'd never started this."

"Take comfort," advised Marionette as she rose from the couch, Brewster and his men closing in on her. "You've won yourself a fair lady. What more do you want?"

"Peace of mind, and the prospect of sleep at night."

"You'll soon have both back again. After all, this is nothing to you. You only came here because you thought solving the riddle of Dora Jones would be entertaining. You said so yourself. You got what you deserved. Only Louis and I ..."

"I still don't understand how you could have stood by and let him do what he did." Regina got up too, stunned and unable to grasp the enormity of what had happened. Louis had seemed so sweet and kind. She still found it impossible to accept the truth. "Couldn't you see what a monster he was? He was criminally insane. Why didn't you stop him? Why?"

"Because I loved him," replied Marionette simply, and lifted her hand to look at what she held in it. For the first time, Regina realised that Mme. Boussard had the silver framed photograph with her. "If you had had a husband like this, wouldn't you have done anything on earth to save him?"

"That ... that is Louis?" Regina was incredulous. "But ..."

"This is Louis when I first met him. Like a god: so perfect that it hurt to look at him. I worshipped him then; I never stopped worshipping him. My last act of passion was to kill him, so that they couldn't drag him away and hang him. I loved him that much, but I don't suppose you'll ever understand."

When Regina and Vere were alone, he said softly:

"Don't grieve, sweetheart. It's over now."

"I know, but it isn't easy to forget. I was so fond of Louis. He was kind and gentle and ..." She broke off abruptly. "But he wasn't, was he?"

"No, he wasn't."

"Love like Marionette's ... it was an obsession ... indecent almost."

He gave a crooked smile.

"It was a grand passion, at least on one side, but remember that if Boussard was insane, so was Marionette in her own way. She was quite mad too. How else could she have endured twenty years shut away in her room, or sheltered a man who killed as easily as he drew breath? No, she was as culpable as he; perhaps more so."

Regina was still ill-at-ease.

"Not everything has been explained, has it?" She glanced round the room as if expecting to find someone else there. "What about the crows? You've heard about them?"

"Yes, but they were pure coincidence. They just happened to settle on Marionette's window sill."

"I don't think so. I believe Rea was right. They came to tell Mme. Boussard of the future, and to warn of death."

"Come, come!"

"Don't dismiss it so lightly, Philippe; I mean Vere. Oh dear, how muddling this is. I shall always think of you as Philippe."

"I don't mind." He put an arm round her, touching her cheek lightly with his lips. "You can think of me in any way you like, as long as you'll marry me."

She tried to laugh.

"I suppose I ought to make a maidenly protest, but I don't think I'm up to it just now. Besides, she was right; I do love you. Not like Marionette loved Louis, but ..."

"Praise be for that."

"And another thing." Quickly she told him of the feeling she had had of being drawn towards Marionette. "That was nothing to do with Louis, was it, nor can it be explained."

"Imagination, or perhaps some form of hypnotism."

"No." This time she was very definite. "It wasn't hypnotism. It was too quick. I knew there was malice in this house as soon as I entered it, and the atmosphere was worst in Marionette's room."

"Bad things were happening here."

"Yes, but not bad in that way. It was different. Not human sin."

He held her close, comforting her.

"You sound just like Rea."

"Do I? Well, perhaps only she and I really sensed something about Marionette Boussard which was not normal. What is more, I don't think she was the only force here. I cannot accept that Conrad Von Heltz would have been so distraught over a mask, whatever sort it was. I think it was something else he saw."

"What else was there?"

Vere was frowning, not liking her pallor.

"There were the puppets."

She whispered it, as if she were half-afraid that they were listening, and he was impatient in his urgent desire to make her put such ideas out of her head.

"Rubbish!"

"No, it isn't. I saw how he looked; you didn't. And they got into the house."

He was brusque.

"Louis brought them in to scare you. Don't you remember what he wrote in his diary?"

She met his disbelief squarely.

"That wasn't what he wrote. What he said was that I was afraid when some of his children came into the house. That's not the same thing at all."

"Stop it! You are an intelligent woman." Vere was growing really angry. "Of course he was responsible. How else could they have got there?"

She didn't answer the question directly, her voice very low.

"Rea said they were tired of the workshop. They wanted to take over the house."

"Damn that girl!" He checked his temper, seeing her genuine distress. "Come, love, we must go. We've got some rather unpleasant news to break to my poor Percival Jones."

At the gate, Regina paused, looking back for the last time at No: 7, Chantry Close. For a second, she thought she saw a small, satisfied face at one of the upper windows, but she wasn't sure enough to mention it to Vere.

It suddenly occurred to her that Marionette had not explained why she had ordered Louis to take the dolls out of the house two years before, but perhaps no explanation was really necessary. They had been her enemies too. She said quietly:

"Soon everyone will be leaving. Denys, Victor, Jeanne, and the servants. I do hope it won't be too difficult for them to manage."

"I don't suppose it will. Denys and Victor will have to work for their living, of course, but that won't hurt them. The servants will probably get other positions easily enough, although what will happen to Jeanne ..."

He broke off, helping her into the carriage, but again she stopped.

"They'll have the place to themselves when the family has gone."

"Regina!" The grip on her arm was almost spiteful. "Will you please be quiet!"

"It's what they've been waiting for all this time." She was as oblivious to his wrath as she was to his tightening hold. "I know that you believe there is a logical explanation for everything which has happened, and perhaps you are right, but somehow I can't quite accept it. There was something about Marionette ... and as for the dolls ... well. All the others will go, but not them. They'll stay here for ever."